P9-CCS-811

THE LAMPFISH OF TWILL

A Richard Jackson Book

The Lampfish of Twill

BY

Janet Taylor Lisle

ILLUSTRATIONS BY

Wendy Anderson Halperin

ORCHARD BOOKS
NEW YORK

Orchard Books
95 Madison Avenue, New York, NY 10016

Manufactured in the United States of America
Book design by Mina Greenstein
The text of this book is set in 12 point Weiss.
The illustrations are pencil drawings reproduced in halftone.
3   5   7   9   10   8   6   4   2

Library of Congress Cataloging-in-Publication Data
Lisle, Janet Taylor.
The lampfish of Twill / by Janet Taylor Lisle ; illustrations by
Wendy Anderson Halperin.   p.   cm.
Summary: An old fisherman leads Eric down a whirlpool to an
ancient and beautiful world in the core of the Earth.
ISBN 0-531-05963-4.   ISBN 0-531-08563-5 (lib. bdg.)
[1. Fantasy.   2. Fishing—Fiction.]
I. Halperin, Wendy Anderson, ill.   II. Title.
PZ7.L6912Lam   1991   [Fic]—dc20   91-8279

In memory of
the good ship *Chivaree*
and
Captain Alden Taylor

Illustrations

then stilled, rippled, then rested. Every bone was visible, every organ and every vein. *page 57*

In an instant, ten strong fishcatchers, including Aunt Opal, sprang up and began to pull the big net up.

page 78

"Ha, ha! We're in it now! There's the surge that stirs the blood. Hold on tight, and we'll steer a bit closer!" *page 98*

"Lampfish!" Eric looked up. He saw them immediately: enormous pink-scaled fish trailing streams of foamy mustaches across Underwhirl's bright sky. *page 121*

The fishcatcher appeared to be conjuring or calling for something. And then Eric saw that he was being answered. One of the lampfish was dropping toward the ground. *page 135*

Eric held Gully gently, so he'd know he didn't have to wait anymore. He could go when he wanted. *page 152*

THE LAMPFISH OF TWILL

1

THE country of Twill lay on the sea, its coastline as treacherous as any in the world. Sharp
claws of rock stretched out from the beaches, and rip-
tides and murderous currents churned the water in-
between.

These currents had carved deep pits in the ocean
floor, where whirlpools howled and sucked from the
water's surface whatever log or buoy or bird chanced
to float within reach. Sometimes a whole ship was lost
in this manner. Over the years, many ships had met
their end along the coast of Twill. Most had gone on
the rocks. Their smashed hulls could be seen dismally
rotting on ledges, a reminder to sailors passing to keep
their own vessels far out to sea. No captain in his right
mind ventured near Twill's coast during the Season of
Storms, which made up half the year. And even during
the relatively peaceful Season of Calm, which was the
year's other half, Twill's one port languished for lack
of trade.

The people of Twickham, as the one port was called, often went without oranges and sugar for months at a time, such was the terrible reputation of their coast. A person who could not make his own soap, went without. Anyone who was too tired at the end of a long day to make candles, or too sad, as the case sometimes was, went to bed early in the dark.

The people of Twickham bore their share of sadness. They were fishing folk and had to deal with their coastline every day. Everyone fished in Twickham— men, women, and children, who were allowed to skip school during the whole Season of Calm, so important was their contribution to the catch. Hardly a month went by when someone wasn't drowned or crushed or battered or crippled or swallowed up by the terrible tides.

They went forth in slim boats designed for scooting between the rocks. They climbed up the rocks from the beach and dangled long baited lines over the ledges. They set traps for crabs near the swirling water's edge. They hurled complicated nets from their cliffs onto seething ocean pools below, whereupon they rushed down the cliffs to pull on certain ropes, which drew the nets through the water and gathered up the fish.

The people of Twickham were ingenious beyond measure in the catching of fish, and they were careful beyond measure to protect themselves from danger. But however ingenious and careful they were, accidents happened. A father was lost to the whirlpools or a mother disappeared under a wave or a brother or sister fell off a rock and was swept by a current to an unseen place. Then black curtains were hung in all the windows of the town, and everyone in Twickham wept for the lost ones. They held one another's hands and brought supper to one another's houses and shared the precious candles so that they could stay up later at night to talk and tell sad stories.

"Who will be next?" they often asked, looking around with fearful eyes. "How can we ever go on?"

Nevertheless, the next day, they did go on. They had to go—back to the rocks, to the boats, to the fishing that was their way of life. There were the hardworking children to be fed, and the babies to be made to grow up strong with fish chowder.

There was the doctor who must eat so that the injured could be tended and returned to work, and the netmakers who must be served so that the important tasks of net weaving and net repair could go on night and day.

There were the gardens to be fertilized with ripe fish heads so that the beans and corn would grow, and the fishhooks to be carved from the red bones of the giant lampfish. And there were a hundred other necessities to be extracted from the daily catch—fish oil and fish tallow, fish glue and fish sauce, fish powder and fish salt—all these so that the people of Twickham might eke out a living, week after week, on the cruel coast of Twill.

2

"**E**RIC," said his aunt Opal very early one morning during the Season of Calm. "I was thinking that you might set the crab traps today on Cantrip's Point. The wind is down a bit, and the tides are running low. I don't suppose you'll fall into any trouble."

"Of course I won't," Eric replied, looking across the breakfast table at his aunt's worn face. "Can I take the big net, too? There's a deep place off the rocks there where I think a lampfish lives."

"A lampfish! Well! We could certainly use some new hooks. By all means, take the net and sound the bell to tell the others. But do be careful, Eric, of the swell around the point. Cantrip's Spout is just offshore and, Season of Calm or not, it's churning in its bed."

"Yes, Aunt," Eric said politely, though he'd heard this warning many times. Everyone in Twickham knew the black boil of water that was the whirlpool off Cantrip's Point. Of all Twill's whirlpools, it was the largest and most treacherous. Its toll in sailing schooners alone stood at four hundred twelve, according to town records. And this didn't include the countless smaller boats swallowed over the years, or the rafts of careless children that had drifted too far out from shore.

Only one person in Twill's history had gone down the spout and come back alive. This was a long-ago man named Cantrip, for whom the whirlpool and nearby point of land were named. How he'd escaped, no one ever found out, because afterward he'd talked in crazy circles and could not be understood. It was said in his day that a person need only whisper "Cantrip's Spout" in his hearing for him to lose sense completely and begin to shriek with laughter.

"Good-bye, then, and keep your eyes open," Aunt Opal said, heading out of their small cottage with a knapsack full of fishing gear slung on her back. She was a skilled fishcatcher who'd learned to fend for herself on Twill's coast and never needed anyone to help her. But one windy day, Eric's parents had gone out fishing and not come home. Though he waited and waited in their cabin by the sea, and kept the kettle hot as he'd been told, they never came to make supper that night, or the next. So Aunt Opal had trudged across the fields and brought him back to live with her.

"I never expected to take on a partner," she'd announced, eyeing him uneasily when they arrived inside her house. "But seeing as you're here and likely to stay, how about going into business with me?"

It was a question most people would consider cold under the circumstances. Eric understood exactly what she meant. There'd be no mothering, no cleaning up after, no complaining, and an equal share of work. He guessed it wasn't the best of all possible worlds, but then again, as lives went in Twill, it wasn't the worst either. He certainly couldn't go back to his empty cabin. When Aunt Opal made her offer, he'd pulled out a bench and sat down quickly in her rough, work-manlike kitchen.

So long ago did this seem now that Eric could barely remember it, and even his parents' faces had become vague moons in his mind, though he would never admit this to anyone. Only his memory of the first blind terror of losing them traveled with him through the years, making him a careful person, a boy who'd rather rely on himself than the plans and promises of others.

Now Eric watched his aunt's long strides as she went off down the road. Night still clung to hollows in the land, for the sun had only just begun to rise. Fishing in Twickham began early and went on till dark, so great was the need of the people.

He watched her turn and call back at the stone gate, "I'll be surf-netting at Dead Man's Beach if you want me. Clap your bell in that direction if the lampfish shows up." A moment later, she vanished down the south road to the coast, and Eric, scanning the sky with a wary eye, wondered what sort of day it would be.

Not such a bad one, maybe, from the look of its beginning, he thought—then wished he hadn't in case it brought a change of luck. You couldn't be too cautious when you lived in Twill. But the sun's first rays

were streaming rosily across the fields. The air was clear
and cool on the skin. A salt breeze blew through hedges
and bush clumps, giving the scene a tossed, flag-waving
look.

Most likely Eric's thoughts weren't the only cheerful
ones on the coast of Twill that morning, because this
was the kind of weather that made spirits rise. The
people of Twickham might live cruel lives most of the
time, but every once in a while a day like this would
come along to put a snap of color in the palest cheek.
Then the coast folk would hail one another on the
roads and smack each other on the back.

"Congratulations!" they would cry. "Many congratulations!" It was the time-honored greeting along the
coast of Twill. "Congratulations" meant "Hello. Nice
to see you." But it also meant, "Well, so we're still here,
you and I, in spite of everything. Congratulations to
us and let's enjoy it while we can!"

As soon as his aunt was gone, Eric turned and went
through the cottage and out the back door. Here, he
paused to check the sky again. This time he seemed
to be looking for something more than good weather.
He ran his eyes slowly around the horizon. With his
foot, he probed a cluster of bushes growing near the
back steps. He glanced up at the cottage roof and then
across the yard to the weather-beaten thatch of an old
tackle shed. Finally, with a frown, he raised two fingers
to his lips and blew one long, shrill whistle.

A flustered noise of something taken by surprise
erupted from the direction of a large woodpile standing

in the yard. It was followed by a rattle of dry leaves, and then a teetery-wobbly sound, as of something losing its balance.

"Qwawk!" A desperate cry broke from somewhere near the top of the woodpile, and at the same moment, a large gray and white body appeared, hurtling down through the air. There was a last, pitiful screech, followed by the sound of a crash landing on hard ground.

Eric thrust his hands in his pockets and looked away in embarrassment.

"So there you are!" he said, fixing his eye on a low-flying cloud. And then, as if not a thing were wrong with this sort of entrance, he added, cheerily,

"Sorry to get you out of bed so early. We're going to Cantrip's today. Remember that lampfish? I was just heading to the tackle shed to get the big net. Have you had breakfast yet? And what do you think of the weather?"

All this silly prattle gave the rumpled, feather-strewn shape at the foot of the woodpile time to gather itself, as Eric certainly intended. What arose from the ungainly heap of wings and bill and eyes and webbed feet was the noble profile of a large sea gull.

Once on its feet, it began to strut around the yard, composing feathers with impatient shrugs and lifting its handsome bill into lordly poses—a little too lordly for good taste, perhaps, but after such a ridiculous fall, who could blame him for trying to improve his appearance?

"Sir Gullstone," Eric murmured respectfully, at

which the sea gull seemed to pull up straighter and to walk with even more terrible dignity. Then Eric held out his arm, which was a signal between them, and the gull flapped his wings twice and landed there. His weight was so great that the boy had to support his one arm with the other.

"Do you remember when you were small enough to sit in my hand?" he asked the bird. His usual guarded look was gone, and his mouth showed the trace of a smile. "You were the smallest, skinniest little orphan gull, and no one expected you to live more than five minutes. You were wet all over and coated with sand from getting rolled up the beach by the surf. Aunt Opal said you were a goner. And Mrs. Holly, who was over for supper, said you were wretched and nasty and to take you out of her sight so she could eat her fish stew.

"Which I didn't do, of course. I wrapped you up in a dish towel and put you near the fire. Do you remember, Gully?"

All the time Eric spoke, the sea gull stared haughtily around the yard and showed no interest in the words lavished upon him. Eric could have been a fence post for all the notice the bird seemed to take of his perch. But at the mention of his pet name, Gully, his heavy yellow bill swung around, and he gazed at Eric with unblinking, adoring, lemon-colored eyes.

"I bet you really don't," Eric said. "I bet you were too little to remember anything, even what your mother looked like, and now you're just pretending because you don't want to admit it."

Sir Gullstone Sea Gull turned his bill away, upon hearing this, and took up such a proud, stiff-legged pose on Eric's arm that he seemed in danger of falling a second time. But Eric, who knew all the difficulties and oddities of his great bird (and one was a tendency to topple off perches), lowered him gently to the ground.

"Come on! We've got to get moving," he announced, glancing up at the sky again. He set out across the yard to the tackle shed, where the big net was stored.

Of all their many pieces of fishing equipment, this one was the heaviest, bulkiest, and most difficult to manage. The big net had a special cart of its own to travel about in, and it was not unusual to see two grown men pushing such a cart along the road to the sea. Inside the shed, Eric grasped the wooden handle of the "net trolley," as it was called, and with a great heave put its wheels in motion. Through the door, across the cottage yard, down a small slope and out to the road the trolley rolled, while Eric ran along behind, guiding it expertly. There he brought it up short without a squeak or a pinch, so that the crab traps could be loaded on. Getting a trolley in motion and keeping it on track was hard, but not so hard as bringing it to a stop. Stopping required precision, a deft flick and yank on the handle to break the wheels' momentum.

With a fine show of skill, Eric halted the trolley just opposite the pile of crab traps near the old stone wall and loaded three of the wooden traps inside. Then, signaling to Sir Gullstone, who looked perilously close to going to sleep again and falling off his own two feet, Eric set off, keeping the big net moving at such a clip along the north road to the coast that there was barely time to exchange a word with the folk he met.

"Congratulations, Eric. Going to Cantrip's today?"

"Many congratulations to you, and yes, I am."

After he had passed, people turned their heads to watch him, since it was unusual for a boy alone to have charge of a big net, and more unusual still that he could manage it so well. And then again, many remembered Eric's mother and father, and the tragedy of their early end.

"That boy's father had a reputation for handling the big net as a youngster," one fishcatcher murmured as Eric thundered past.

"For all the good it did him," muttered another, with a shake of his head.

From above, the bleating cry of a coastal gull pierced the air, but neither fishcatcher bothered to look up. Only Eric, hearing the sound from further along the road, shot a worried glance over his shoulder. Sir Gullstone was all right, though. He was following at his own pace, embroidering his flight with elegant swoops and curlicues. No bird on the coast flew more beautifully, Eric thought with a surge of pride. It was amazing how all sign of the sea gull's earthbound awkwardness vanished the moment he took to the sky. Gone, too, were the strutting and fluffing and vain posturing. Gully looked so breathtaking up there with the morning light flashing off his wings that Eric wished he could stop for a moment to watch.

No time for that, though. There was never any time for breathtaking moments in Twill. There was always the fishing and trapping, the netting and scaling to be done, and in between, the nervous eye to be kept open for a change of weather. Eric knew the rules as well as anyone.

"Faster!" he shouted to the great wheeling form overhead. "Stop that fooling around. The sun's almost up! Hurry or we'll miss the . . ." and he lowered his voice.

"Lampfish," he whispered, because it was not the sort of word a person went around yelling, especially if wanting to catch one.

3

AMPFISH. They were an ancient class of fish, large and round as waterwheels and, with their watery green eyes and foamy mustaches, by far the strangest creatures off Twill's coast. They were also the most difficult to catch. While other fishes' bodies were covered with bronze or silver scales, the lampfish's scales shone rosy pink. This was protective coloration. Ever alert to danger and modest in their tastes, lampfish never ventured from their underwater holes during broad daylight. They were dawn and evening feeders, appearing at those times when the sun's rising and setting cast their special lampfish red upon the water.

Then, for a few minutes, they wallowed cautiously, and almost invisibly, in clumps of sea grass growing outside their holes. They nibbled algae that grew on the stalks. But the moment the light changed, they withdrew, and nothing would lure them out again, as the fishcatchers of Twickham knew well.

There was another time the prehistoric fish left their

holes, but it did the fishcatchers no good at all. Dark windless nights, those nights on which the sky was clear but the moon never rose, were called lampfish nights along the coast of Twill. Then the lampfish emerged and swam about the coastal waters for hours at a time. They drifted among rocks and into currents that no Twickham resident would dare go near after dark, that were risky enough by day, heaven knew. They floated maddeningly hither and yon, quite visible to the folk on land because they glowed like red lamps under the black night water.

Lampfish. It was amazing how powerful the light of these creatures was. Their glow illuminated the sea for many feet around them. And not only was the water lit up, but the inside of the lampfish was clearly revealed by its own queer, pinkish light—stomach, esophagus, heart, brain, and especially a fine network of the precious red bones that all Twickham prized for the making of fishhooks.

Eric's thoughts about lampfish were especially vivid on the road that morning because of the fish he had seen only two days before at Cantrip's Point. Twice the usual size it had seemed when it appeared suddenly, floating in the water off the rocks at dusk. He'd been crouched on a ledge, trying to mend a small net that had snagged and torn during the day. Quickly, he'd rolled onto his stomach and peered over the ledge just in time to see the enormous body pass directly beneath him, trailing mustaches like long silken scarves.

The creature rubbed dreamily against an underwater rock. Then, with the unhurried grace of a descending hot air balloon, it began to sink. Its form became a pink ripple under the water, then a shadow. A minute later, it disappeared into a dark place under the ledge.

Not for several minutes did Eric stir. So unusual was it to come upon a lampfish hole, to actually see a lampfish entering its secret home, that he completely forgot about the net he was mending. And when he finally did lift himself off his stomach, he simply sat on the rock and stared out to sea.

It is well-known on Twill's coast that no fishcatcher can look at a lampfish without wanting to catch it. No sooner is one of the giant floaters spotted than the spotter rings a bell to signal those fishing nearby. Lampfish are too big and too fierce to catch alone, so every fishcatcher carries a powerful hand bell as part of the regular gear. Eric's bell, which had been his mother's, and his grandmother's before, was stowed, at that moment, in an unused crab trap lying behind him on the rock. He knew he should jump up and go get it. But he didn't. Instead, he looked over at Gully, who was nestled nearby on a tuft of grass.

"This lampfish certainly lives in a convenient place," he remarked in a casual voice.

There was a pause, during which Sir Gullstone located a pesky gull louse under the feathers of one wing, and swallowed it decisively.

"You know what?" Eric went on. "I bet we could catch this fish by ourselves if we wanted to."

The sea gull's bill came around at this, and his lemon eyes seemed to examine, doubtfully, the thinness of his friend's arms, the knobbiness of his knees. Perhaps they even peered inside his skull to detect a lunatic band of brain cells there.

"Stop looking at me! I bet we could!" Eric protested. But he added immediately, "If we were crazy enough to try."

He understood the risks all too well. Through the years, the number of lampfish netted by a single pair of hands amounted to pitifully few. Everyone in Twickham knew the names of the heroes who had done it. As for those who had tried and failed—those drowned in their own nets or throttled by their own lines or beaten senseless by a fish's thrashing body—their names sank and vanished into Twill's bottomless past.

What with all the dangers faced daily by people on the coast, the idea of choosing to hunt lampfish alone looked foolish to most. Moreover, it looked arrogant. To go specially courting trouble when everybody else was trying specially to avoid it showed the worst sort of pride.

Once the thing had been done, though, once a lampfish had been caught, Twickham folk were so awestruck that they forgot to be angry. They raised the catcher up on their shoulders and marched him or her around town.

They threw a great feast and celebration in honor of the survivor, whose name was engraved on a plaque on the town commons.

"Con-grat-ul-ations!" they screamed and sang and chanted. Many had tears in their eyes. Then the bones of the lampfish, the rare and wonderful lampfish that had been caught by a single pair of hands, were put aside for safekeeping. Much as the town needed fishhooks, these bones were kept apart. They were carved into the figures of famous Twillian fishcatchers, and also into scenes depicting the great lampfish hunts in history, so that the heroes and their stories would never be forgotten.

Never . . . be . . . forgotten. Eric stared into the water off the ledge. He wasn't greedy or conceited or foolish. Of course he wasn't. But:

"This fish really wouldn't be that hard to catch," he had found himself explaining to Gully that afternoon at Cantrip's Point. "His hole is right under us. Look, you can see it yourself. All we'd have to do is roll the big net down here and drop it over."

He'd explained it so many times (while Gullstone kept on looking doubtful—he could be a most stupid bird sometimes!) that at last Eric had been late for supper, which made Aunt Opal cross because it was his turn to do the cooking. . . .

Out on the north road, Eric spat on his hands and drove the net trolley hard around a rugged curve. For two days he'd kept the hole at Cantrip's Point a secret, turning over various problems in his head. Now a perfect day had dawned, and he knew he'd have to try for the lampfish alone.

Ahead, the land flattened out and water came into

view. The sun was just up. It hung low and red in the sky, like a great lampfish itself floating over the silver sea. A stream of rosy light poured from it, straight across the waves to Eric.

The road crossed several open fields before its final plunge to Cantrip's Point. Eric hurtled over one field, passed through a second, and was well into the last when he realized with a gulp that his mind had wandered. The trolley was approaching the plunge too fast. There was no time to change course.

The cart struck the slope's crest with an earsplitting whack. It soared for several feet through the air, hitting the hill's downward side at a tremendous rate of speed. Eric was yanked off his feet. Somehow, he managed to right himself in back of the trolley. Then he dug his heels into the dirt to try to brake the cart. A spume of dust poured out behind him. The big net roared downhill. Only a few feet above the ledge, it came to a shrieking stop.

Eric wiped the dirt out of his eyes and looked around in embarrassment to see if anyone had been watching. Luckily, the distant rocks seemed clear of fishcatchers. Even Gullstone had been left behind. The sky was empty. Eric was about to whistle for him when a faint gurgling sound caught his ear from the water under the ledge. He crept forward on the rock to see what was there.

Below, a huge lampfish wallowed in seaweed. Perhaps the creature had been alarmed by the noise of the net trolley crashing downhill. It had stopped feeding and seemed to be waiting or listening for something. But shortly, it resumed the gentle nibbling of weed stalks that is the manner of all lampfish. Its mustaches twirled and spun in the waves. The rosy scales of its great round back blended perfectly with the rosy morning light. Eric never could have seen it if he had not been looking directly down. He let his breath out and tiptoed away to fetch the big net.

"Yo-ho! Congratulations there!"

The shout made him jump and whirl around.

"Yo-ho! Almost lost your trolley overboard, and yourself as well, I see!" a voice crowed joyously. "I was watching from Strangle Point, next one up. Thought for a minute you weren't going to make it!"

Eric flushed. "Of course I was going to make it." He scowled at the approaching figure.

It was an old fishcatcher, a truly antique specimen from the look of his rubber boots and his long tarpaulin coat. No one wore things like that anymore. He came swaying across the field like a ship before the wind, and when he got to Eric, he rapped him rudely on the chest.

"I said I wasn't sure you'd make it!" he shouted again. "There've been some accidents on this place. Don't think there haven't!"

"I'm sure there have," Eric answered, with a furious glance toward the ledge. "And thanks for coming over, but I'm all right, as you see. So you can go back to—"

"What'd you say?" howled the fellow. He was deaf as an old dog. Eric mopped his brow with a hand. On second thought, he dried the hand on his pants and held it out to the fishcatcher, whose own sea-wrinkled paw rose to meet it.

"Thanks!" Eric yelled at the aged ears. "And good-bye!" he shouted, shaking the paw with extra vigor. The oilskin coat exuded a musky, tarlike odor, and creaked whenever its occupant moved. It must weigh a ton, Eric thought.

The fishcatcher grinned. "Not at all. Not at all! Glad to be on deck. There's dark water off this point, you can bet your cleats and battens."

He really was an old man. He used phrases and bits of speech that had been out of fashion in Twill for years, that Eric had only read about in old books.

"Dark water?" Eric repeated. "If you mean the whirlpool, everyone knows about that."

"Aye, the spout, the spout. That's as grand a spout as ever was. Some say there's more to it than what appears. Some believe it don't stop at the ocean floor, but digs down through the earth and comes out the other side."

The fishcatcher winked. "Where'd it come out, would you say, if it did come out someplace else?"

Eric shrugged. "China?"

The old fellow laughed.

"I'd put my bet down on a place a whole lot farther off than that," he said, and winked mysteriously again.

"There's nowhere farther off than China," Eric replied. "China's exactly halfway around the world from Twill. You can't go any farther and still be on the earth."

"That depends on who's doing the traveling, and where and how, don't it?" the old fishcatcher said.

Eric was about to ask what this was supposed to mean when he saw the fellow glance up at the sky. Though it looked perfectly clear and blue, the fishcatcher gestured and began to back away.

"Will you take a glint of that!" he cried. "Dirty weather coming in. I'll be getting back to my traps. You'd best pack up that big net of yours and head off home. The morning's broke for fishing, I'd say. Aye, broke as a boat on the rocks of Twill."

This was such an old-fashioned expression that Eric couldn't help smiling as the fishcatcher staggered away across the fields toward Strangle Point. The man was a little daft. There wasn't a cloud in the sky for as far as Eric could see, and the breeze had dropped to almost nothing. The ocean rocked peacefully around the point. Waves ruffled over the spot where the big whirlpool churned, several hundred yards offshore. Otherwise, nothing moved, nothing squawked, not a murmur or a gurgle could be heard from the water.

Not a gurgle! Eric ran for the edge of the rocks. He peered over and then flung himself on his stomach and craned his neck far out over the ledge. The long weeds were still there, swirling underwater, but the lampfish was gone. While the fishcatcher had prattled on, the light had changed. The creature had gone back into its hole.

Eric turned and glared in the direction of Strangle Point. Now he'd have to wait all day for the light to be right again, and with no guarantee that the fish would return. Who was that idiot fishcatcher anyway? The old blatherer, the walking tar-skin—

A shadow moved across the sun. Looking up, Eric saw a bank of black clouds surging up the sky from the horizon. The clouds billowed and blew forward like tremendous capes, swirling over one another, swallowing each other up. The whole eastern half of the sky became one sweep of churning black, and then, as Eric watched in amazement, the sun was attacked and swallowed, too.

"Gullstone! Gullstone! The weather's changing!" he cried. He ran along the ledge, waving his hands. The sea gull was nowhere in sight.

"Gully!" The wind started to blow. In the trolley, the crab traps began to rattle and then to jump and slam together. Still the bird would not come. Eric knew he must wait no longer. The storm was closing in with a speed unusual even for Twill's coast, and from its looks, it was a bad one.

Zot! Zing! There, away low on the horizon, Eric saw the first flickers of electrical activity as he raced for the trolley. He tucked the wooden handle up over the big net, jammed the crab traps tighter inside, and began the laborious job of pushing the cart backwards uphill. The road back from Cantrip's was always a hard one, especially the first climb to the fields above. Eric threw his weight against the trolley and heaved it up the slope with all his strength.

"Gully!" he yelled, whenever he had breath, but his voice was drowned out by the roar of the storm.

Across the water it streaked like a black-winged

dragon, rumbling, hissing, breathing out tongues of fire. Halfway up the hill, Eric turned to look back. He glanced over to Strangle Point. Mountainous waves were crashing onto the beach and hurling themselves up the ledges into the fields.

"Gully! Please come!" Wind and salt spray pelted his eyes. He wondered how the poor hobbling fish-catcher would ever get his traps, or himself, stowed away in time.

4

ERIC'S aunt was already home when he arrived, wringing wet and with his hair whipped across his face.

"Gullstone's still out," he told her breathlessly. "He disappeared on the way to Cantrip's Point and never came back."

Aunt Opal sighed. "Go sit by the fire," she said. "I'll watch for him. You look half blown away."

She went to stand by the window. Outside, the wind shrieked along the road, bending bushes into crazy, streaming shapes.

"It's a tempest sent straight from the Season of Storms," she observed, while Eric peeled off his wet jacket. "The Old Blaster couldn't wait for his turn to come around, so he's showing us a bit of his stuff beforetime. It's nasty of him, all right."

Eric nodded. The Old Blaster was what people along the coast called bad weather during the Season of Storms. Or rather, they saw the weather's fury and violence during those months as issuing from a single, brutal personality. The Old Blaster was vengeful, malicious, and uncaring. He wreaked havoc whenever he could, sparing no one, not the smallest child or the weakest old person. He was often tricky and unpredictable. Sometimes he'd lie low for weeks just to drive up the suspense. Then he'd attack full force and scare the daylights out of people.

This storm, appearing from nowhere, certainly had all the earmarks of The Old Blaster, Eric thought, as he put on a dry shirt in a back room of the cottage. He wasn't sure he really believed, as many in Twickham did, that a powerful old man who lived beyond the horizon was in charge of making life miserable for people. Still, he wasn't sure he didn't believe, either, especially when it might make The Blaster angry to find out he was doubted.

"Any sign of Gully?" he called to his aunt. "He probably can't fly in this wind. I just hope he can walk."

"Nothing yet," she shouted back. "I've brewed some hot tea, when you're ready. I was thinking we ought to go lend a hand at the harbor. They're trying to haul the boats from the water before dark. It's rumored the wind will go to hurricane force tonight.

"And your bird's not the only one who hasn't come home," she added, when Eric sat down at the table with his tea mug. "There's a fishing boat still out."

She didn't look around at him. She kept her eyes on the window.

"Whose is it?"

"Granger's, they say."

"Granger! Harold Granger? But Mrs. Granger was killed in a riptide just last month. Are Joey and Rachel with him?"

"No one knows about the children."

Outside, a shutter had come loose. It began to bang against the side of the house, and Eric couldn't help thinking how sometimes in Twill it seemed that everything was about to fly apart, that it was no good trying to keep things nailed down because the wind got them eventually, or the sea did. And maybe someday, some last evil day, The Old Blaster would tire of his ancient game against them and send one final, horrible blast. Then, everything in Twill would be swept off the land and drowned in the sea forever.

"I hope Rachel and Joey are on the boat," Eric said bitterly, when he had listened to the shutter a while longer. "Then, whatever happens, at least their whole family will be in it together."

Aunt Opal glanced around at him. "No one should wish for such a thing," she replied. "How could anyone wish for such a terrible thing?" She looked at him hard before turning back to the window.

"That is no shutter beating against my house," she added after several moments.

"What is it?"

"Something with a screech."

"A screech!"

Eric listened. There amidst the banging and the

howl of wind and thrashing of bushes came another noise:

"Qwawk!" And again, "Qwawk, qwawk!"

"It's Gully," he screamed. "Open the door! Let him in!"

He leaped to the door and flung it open himself. The big sea gull blew against him, and past, into the cabin on a violent gust of wind.

"Close up before we're blown to smithereens!" bellowed Aunt Opal. So Eric hurled himself upon the door a second time and, after a struggle, managed to latch it shut.

In the relative calm that followed, both turned their eyes upon Sir Gullstone, who had fallen to the ground like a shot goose the moment the door was closed. Never had they seen such a tangle of feathers, or such a twisting of wing and neck on a living bird. It seemed that the sea gull must be dead, that the pile of pieces on the floor before them could not possibly be brought together to work again.

But then, a yellow bill moved with an impatient thrust. And two arrogant legs poked testily at the ground. Next, a body was hoisted upon them, a pair of lemon eyes blinked open, and the whole contraption began to limp with lordly strides toward the fire's warmth.

"Oh, Gully," whispered Eric. "You are perfectly all right!" He heaved a tremendous sigh of relief and ran over to throw his arms around the precious bird.

Aunt Opal, however, turned back to the window

with a shake of her head. "We'll not be going to the harbor after all," she said grimly. "It's clear that the wind has grown too strong for us to be of help to anyone now."

FOR TWO DAYS, the storm ravaged and ransacked the coastline of Twill. Then it blew out to sea with such ghastly shrieks and moans that the noise could be heard for hours echoing back across the water.

In its aftermath, the town of Twickham lay stricken under a pallid morning sun. For a long while, no one dared come out of the house. The only sound in the streets was the dripping of eaves and, from the beaches below, the growling of still-maddened waves.

When people did come forth at last, they gathered in groups to whisper on salt-spattered corners. They pointed to the doors ripped from hinges and the chimneys toppled from the roofs. They showed one another the smashed windows, the fallen lampposts, the drowned cat bobbing in the sewer.

But there was worse.

"There's always worse on the coast of Twill," Mrs. Holly said to Aunt Opal, after they'd met and warily congratulated each other on the road to town. "If you and Eric are going to the weep tonight at Grangers', would you mind me walking with you? It's not a time to be alone."

"No, it isn't," replied Aunt Opal. "We'd be glad to pick you up on our way by." Together, the women looked off across the fields to where Twill's coast came into view. And though the sea appeared there as the meekest and most charming pool of blue, their faces hardened.

Harold Granger's fishing boat had never come home. One glance at the rocks off the coast showed the reason. The hull lay crushed on Mad Bull, a ledge that had been the death of many good crews over time, and many strong sailing ships. There was no disgrace in ending there, the Granger children were assured.

They were orphans, now: eight-year-old Rachel, with a pair of braids thicker than her wrists; bowlegged Joey, ten, who wore his fishing cap backwards and liked to kid around. Eric knew them from school. Neither had been with their father on the morning of the storm. For this, the people of Twickham raised thankful eyes to the east, where The Blaster was generally believed to hole up.

"Though why we bother thanking the old tyrant, it's hard to see," Aunt Opal remarked, as she, Mrs. Holly, and Eric trudged the muddy road to town that evening. "Everybody knows he would have drowned the children, too, if he could have got them."

"Hush!" said Mrs. Holly, tucking a dish towel more firmly around the cake she was carrying in a basket. "You never know who's listening!"

"Has anyone gone to look at the Grangers' boat?" Eric asked. "Maybe Mr. Granger is still hanging on out there. He was a smart fishcatcher. I can't believe he isn't somewhere around."

"Someone has gone, and he isn't," Mrs. Holly replied, drawing a ragged breath. "And please let's not speak of it anymore."

In Twill, it was the case that those lost at sea were rarely found, whether because of The Blaster or the treacherous currents offshore. In fact, Mrs. Holly's husband had disappeared in just this way, not to mention Eric's parents, and the walkers now fell silent to respect these disturbing memories.

Everyone in town tried to cram themselves into the Grangers' house that night. When the three arrived, candles were burning five deep in the windows, casting a waxy glow upon clusters of damp faces. It was obvious that the weep, as these all-too-frequent gatherings had come to be called, was already well under way.

They were half funeral rite, half worship ceremony to The Blaster. Guests were welcome to weep whatever way they wished—with happiness for the miracle of their own survival or with sorrow for those gone. And many wept both ways under the nervous flickers of the fish tallow candles, because their feelings were rather confused.

There was also the important matter of the food. Like Mrs. Holly, most families in Twickham had cooked for the Grangers' weep. Pies, cakes, cookies, casseroles, fish roasts, and oyster stews were piled on every available table and ledge. Eric sniffed the rich smells, but he tasted nothing. Not one guest was eating, nor would anyone touch a scrap, because this was The Blaster's feast alone. At a later hour, it would be taken out and hurled off the Twickham cliffs into the sea. Here, it was hoped, The Blaster would find it and, after filling his cavernous belly, feel inclined to go away nicely, perhaps to sleep for several weeks, and give the town time to recover.

"Do you sometimes wonder if The Old Blaster really does eat our food?" Eric whispered to Mrs. Holly as she placed her cake carefully among the other offerings. Aunt Opal had dumped off a jar of pickled turnips and gone to talk fish nets in the kitchen. "Do you think all this cooking for him does a bit of good?"

Mrs. Holly silenced him with a ferocious glance.

"You are as bad as your aunt about saying what you shouldn't!" she hissed. "You'll be drowned next storm if you keep it up!"

He wasn't the only one saying things, though. Around them, conversations begun in whispers and sniffs were taking a daring turn. People asked why The Blaster had gone after Harold Granger, of all people, and in the Season of Calm as well. Harold was a fine man. A very talented person. What had he done to deserve such treatment? It was outrageous, people said, and too much to bear. Too much for a town to stand anymore. Too much to go on, yes, too much.

Eric listened to these heated words, but he knew they meant little. People always grew angry at weeps. Nothing ever came of it. When the next day dawned clear, or rainy, or even windy, they dragged out their nets and crab traps again. They climbed on their slim boats and rowed through the rocks to go fishing. Tomorrow would be no different. Even the Granger children would go, brave and solemn eyed, on a neighbor's boat.

Eric glanced over to where Joey Granger was standing in a throng of weepers. The boy's face was swollen, and he looked as lost and alone as if he'd been stranded on a desert island. Eric supposed he should go over to him. He should go and say something to make Joey feel better. It was expected in Twill. It was what people had done for him. He didn't go, though. He felt too disgusted. He turned and pushed through the crowd to the Grangers' front door. When no one was looking, he let himself out.

"I had to get away from there, Gully," he told the bird later, as they lay together near the fire. "I couldn't stand it anymore. There was nothing I could say that would've made any difference. Everyone in Twickham gets hit sooner or later. You know it. I know it. We all grew up knowing it. What can anyone do? This is the coast of Twill."

5

Now, for many days, a thick gray mist lay over the coast, as if The Blaster himself thought he'd gone a bit too far and wished to hide Twill's pain from his eyes. Eric went often to Cantrip's Point with the crab traps, where he caught little enough in the gloomy fog. Whenever he went, he brought the big net, though lugging it back and forth was a terrible job. He kept his eye on the lampfish hole at lampfish feeding times, but he never saw anything there.

At first, he thought the big fish might have been frightened off by the storm. Then, when there was still no sign after a week, he wondered if it had been hurt, or perhaps even killed. Lampfish were not known for abandoning their holes.

"But how many holes have been discovered so close to shore?" he said one day to Gullstone, whom he now kept near him at all times by means of a long string tied around the bird's foot. "For that matter, what does anyone in Twickham really know about these fish?

"Will you please stop pecking that string!" he added crossly to the sea gull. "You know it's only for your own good. You don't want to get lost in another of The Blaster's storms, do you?"

Oddly enough, very little was known about lampfish, Eric found, when he began to ask around.

"You aren't supposed to know," a fishcatcher down at the docks told him. "It's too dangerous to try finding out. Lampfish are lampfish, and what they do is their business. I wouldn't worry about it. Just keep an eye open and ring your bell if you see one. There's been only one lampfish caught this year. Everyone in town is in need of fresh hooks."

So Eric kept up his watch over the underwater hole. When the weather cleared, he began to linger at Cantrip's Point after sunset in hopes of catching the big fish on a night expedition. One evening, as he sat on the ledge staring out to sea, and as Gully limped gloomily around in the dark hunting for snails, a shape loomed up and the ancient fishcatcher from Strangle Point appeared. The fellow lurched toward them like a sailor walking the deck of a sinking ship. His tarpaulin coat slapped at his knees.

"Congratulations!" His voice boomed through the night air, loud enough to alert every lampfish for miles around. Eric raised a finger to his lips, but the old man didn't see this, or chose to ignore it. With a great flap of coat and boots, he swung himself to the ground.

"It's a lampfish night if I ever saw one!" he bellowed, waving an arm at the ocean before them. "No moon. No wind. No waves. Seen anything out there yet?"

He looked sharply at Eric. But when the boy shook his head, his old eyes wandered off again and his vacant expression returned. He lay back on his elbows and gazed across the water.

"You never know with lampfish," he murmured. "And that's saying the least of it."

This was so exactly what Eric had been thinking, lately, that he couldn't help but agree with a friendly nod.

They sat together in silence. Eric didn't mind. The night was a pleasant one. When at last the red glows of the lampfish began to rise and glimmer around the point, a sweet feeling of mystery swept through him.

"You were right about that storm coming," he said, turning to the weathered profile beside him. "How'd you know? There wasn't a cloud anywhere, and no wind."

The fishcatcher didn't answer. Perhaps he hadn't heard. Eric didn't want to shout at him. He leaned back and looked up at the sky.

Without the moon, the stars seemed to shine brighter. Far away to the south, an arc of bright light bulged up on the horizon. Eric knew it came from one of the big trading cities some hundred miles below Twill, one of the cities whose lights burned night and day, it was said. No one Eric knew had ever been there to see if this was true. The sea between was too rough for Twickham's slim fishing boats, and even if it hadn't been, Twill folk weren't about to take chances.

Trading ships from the outside brought occasional information. But the foreign sailors who landed at

Twickham were a rowdy, hard-drinking bunch who could not be trusted to tell a sober fact. It was impossible to know whether the buildings in these cities really were made of glass, as one sailor had reported, or if the inhabitants wore furs and jewels and never needed to fish at all, as another had said.

Eric sighed. Beside him, the fishcatcher rustled in his oilskin coat. Sir Gullstone was invisible in the dark. His string had stopped moving. The bird was probably asleep at the end of it, lovable old thing.

"Do you ever think about going someplace else?" Eric suddenly found himself asking the old man. "Because I do. Don't tell my aunt, but I'd like to quit all this fishing. Where does it lead us, anyhow? I want to get off this coast and go someplace where a person can do things without looking over his shoulder all the time, where people aren't being hurt or killed every other day of the week."

Eric gave the string an affectionate shake and glanced at the fishcatcher, who seemed this time to have heard him. He was nodding his head and grinning.

"I've been!" he announced, cheerfully. "It's the same, everywhere!"

"The same! But it couldn't be!"

"It is," said the old man. "Well, up here anyway." He peered at Eric. "Don't think you can keep a thing safe by tying a string around it neither. Can't be done, no. Won't never work."

"What do you mean!" Eric cried, holding fast to Gully's leash. He was about to demand a full explanation when the old man sat up. He cocked his head to one side, listening. He lifted his beakish nose and sniffed the air.

"What is it?" Eric asked. Then he heard something, too. A gentle bubbling sound was coming from the ocean below. A noise of swirling water arose with it, then stopped, then came again. Eric leaped to his feet, but the fishcatcher moved quicker and caught his arm.

"Where are you going?" he snapped. "Stay with me. You can't leave me down here on the ground by myself."

"I won't. I'm just going to see what's making that noise," said Eric, trying to pull his arm away.

The old man held fast. "Don't leave me!" he cried. "Stay here. You can't go."

"Yes, I can!" Eric replied. "I know what's making that noise and I want to see it."

"Noise?" A sly look crossed the fishcatcher's face. "What noise? I don't hear anything. Listen. There's nothing."

He cupped an ear with one hand while with the other he kept hold of Eric. He was strong, much stronger than he looked.

Eric paused and listened, and at first it was true. There were no bubbling sounds. But in the next minute, he heard a great gush of water, as if a wave had broken on a rock, and the sound of something moving away through the sea.

"Let go!" Eric cried, twisting his arm hard in the fishcatcher's grasp. He pulled frantically and, after a second wrench, broke free and raced for the brink of the ledge. He was in time to see only a blazing streak of red far-off in the water near the whirlpool's surge. The color was so intense that he caught his breath. As he watched, the streak was joined by others, in different fiery hues, and a fantastic swirl of lights shone up from the sea and lit the dark water all around.

"Oh!" Eric gasped. "Look! Look!"

A deep sigh came from behind him. He turned to find the fishcatcher raised on his knees, gazing past him in awe.

"It's only the lampfish," Eric reminded him. "You don't have to be afraid."

"Afraid?" The fishcatcher's eyes darted at him angrily. "Only the lampfish, did you say? And tomorrow you'll run to ring your blasted bell, no doubt. First thing in the morning you'll call the whole town out."

"No, I won't," Eric answered. "I could have done that weeks ago."

"So you could." The old man nodded. "I've had my eye on you." He sat back on his heels and squinted at Eric. "This lampfish you've been watching is a fair-sized fish, I think."

"It's a huge one," Eric replied. "And very tricky. I've been after it since before the big storm."

"Its hole, I suppose, is somewhere near here?" The fishcatcher gestured around the point. "And no doubt you've been plotting to land it alone. I must say, I'm disappointed. I'd have wagered you were smarter than that."

"Its hole is right under this ledge, if you want to

know," Eric replied testily. "And what I'm planning to do is no business of yours. Anyway, the fish is out circling Cantrip's Spout right now, so I guess we might as well pack up and go home."

"Cantrip's Spout, did you say? Aha, Cantrip's Spout!"

A strange thing happened to the fishcatcher's mouth. It quivered. Then it wriggled. Then it snaked itself around into a horrid, mirthless grin.

"Cantrip's Spout!" The mouth opened crookedly at one side to let out a splutter. No, it was a giggle. Another giggle followed, and then a full-fledged gurgling laugh. The old man clamped his hand over this terrible mouth, but he could not stop more laughs from boiling up. He bent over gasping and crowed with laughter. He hooted and howled, and held on to his stomach. He rolled on the ground and stuffed his fists between his lips and still he could not stop laughing. Tears streamed from his eyes, and his ancient, sun-bronzed cheeks turned red.

"What's wrong with you?" Eric shouted.

The fishcatcher only laughed harder.

"Stop it! Stop!"

The words had no effect whatever. Eric backed away, off the ledge. An appalling idea had come to him. He thought he knew who this fishcatcher was.

The figure on the ledge continued its horrible, twisting motions. The laughter came in chuckles, then in gulps, then died down, perhaps simply from lack of breath.

"Mr. Cantrip?" Eric called. "Mr. Cantrip, is that you?"

The writhing ceased. The old man's head came up. He looked around, then focused on Eric.

"Cantrip?" he asked.

"Yes. That's who you are, isn't it?" Eric shouted.

With a great creaking of tarpaulin, the fishcatcher rolled again to his knees. He hoisted himself, leg by ancient leg, to his feet. He leaned over and brushed himself off. Sand and debris had caught on his coat. His long white hair had fallen over his eyes. He smoothed it back with both hands and nodded.

"Aye, it's Cantrip, poor devil. It's him. And why he's back standing on this evil point, I don't know. He should never have come. It stirs him up, see. It makes him remember."

He wobbled forward several steps, then stopped and looked back over his shoulder at the black ocean spreading away from the ledge. Eric saw his mouth twitch, again. But the old man drew himself up and began to lumber toward the field.

"I'll be off," he muttered. "It's getting late."

He walked a bit, then turned on Eric.

"I've seen you watching out here for lampfish," he said in a low voice that was clear and perfectly sane. "I know what you've got in your mind. Don't do it, young fellow, that's all I've got to say. Don't go bothering those beautiful fish. And don't be ringing that horrid bell of yours, neither. There's systems at work you know nothing about. Keep yourself moored and battened is my advice, and I know very well what I mean in this case."

All the time he spoke, his eyes were fastened on Eric's. Afterward, he resumed his weird gait through the long grass, heading in the direction of Strangle Point. Eric watched him go with a shiver. He felt cold all over, suddenly, as if some unearthly hand had gripped him and let him go. Only when the figure had vanished into the dark and the creak of tarpaulin had completely died away, did he dare to call softly,

"Gullstone! Wake up! Let's get out of here."

He gave the string a little tug to stir the sleeper.

"Come on! We've got to go. Aunt Opal will be wondering where we are."

There being still no movement, Eric jerked the string harder. It gave way with sickening ease.

"Gullstone!" he shrieked, charging into the dark, but it was too late. Out in the field, the string's end hung limply between clumps of grass. There was no sign whatever of the big sea gull.

6

"A STRANGE man, yes, but not a thief, I think," Aunt Opal said in answer to Eric's urgent question at breakfast the next morning. "Actually, I'm astounded to hear he's still alive."

She paused to watch her nephew ladle her up a steaming bowl of fishmeal. It was his week to make breakfast and do the washing up. She was in charge of dinner and stoking the wood stove. Next week, they'd switch jobs, according to a schedule they had followed from their earliest months together.

"Ezekiel Cantrip's his name," Aunt Opal went on, when Eric had served himself. "Zeke, people used to call him. He was an old fellow even when your father and I were children, and that was years after the spout spat him back."

"He looks about two hundred years old now," Eric said. "And he wears oilskins the way the old-time fish-catchers did."

Aunt Opal nodded. "I remember," she said. "Nobody wanted to get near him because he acted so oddly, whispering to himself, muttering, ignoring what people said to him. And then he'd go into one of his wild fits of laughing. People kept their young ones away whenever he came into town for his groceries. They'd call their dogs home. He'd been a traveler, you know, even before his run-in with the spout, so there was fear on that account as well."

"A traveler?" Eric looked up from his bowl.

"Oh, yes. He left Twill for months at a time, sailed to the trading cities with the traders. And beyond. It made you think twice when you saw him. You wondered what sort of strange ideas he had stored in his head."

"He has some strange idea about the lampfish," Eric said. "He doesn't like us hunting them. Twice he's come bothering me when he thinks I've gotten too close. And the way he looks at me, it gives me the shivers."

Aunt Opal smiled. "When I was small, there was a story passed among the children that old Zeke had unusual powers and could put a spell on you if you looked him in the eye. Some even believed he was related to The Blaster. Of course we all ran away when we saw him coming. And because he frightened us, we used to yell things at him. Nasty things, I'm afraid. He didn't seem quite human, you see."

"Maybe he isn't," Eric replied. "He predicts things, and they come true. It's almost as if he had some way of making them happen. He predicted the big storm."

"In Twill, anyone can do that," said Aunt Opal. "I

can predict a big storm right now, and it's sure to happen. Maybe tomorrow, in fact. The Season of Storms is nearly upon us."

"Well, Mr. Cantrip predicted his storm five minutes before it came out of a clear blue sky. And last night he all but told me that Gullstone might escape. And now he has!"

Eric got up and went to look out the dim window for the tenth time that morning. "Unless Gully got put under some mysterious spell himself, and stolen," he added, darkly.

"If I were a bird and someone tied me up at the end of a string, I'd try to escape, too," Aunt Opal pointed out. "And eventually, I'd succeed. There's no mystery in that."

It was all she had time to say because Twill's red sun appeared on the horizon at that moment, and worries over the day's catch pulled her thoughts away.

"Please pay attention to your crab traps today and not to that idiot gull, who is bound to turn up when he wants and not a minute before," she told Eric, rather severely, as she left. "We've fallen behind our usual catch totals and must work harder than ever if we're to save enough to last through the bad season."

But Eric stood on by the window after she had gone, hoping to glimpse a familiar pair of wings. He went out back of the cottage and whistled and shouted into the vacant sky. The sun rose up, a brisk southwest wind took charge of the day, and still no sea gull appeared.

He was wasting precious time, he knew, and he

began to feel guilty. Aunt Opal would be furious if she came back and found him there. Actually, he was furious at himself. There was no excuse for this kind of hanging around. Gully would come back. He always came back. And if he didn't come back . . . well? Well, what? Eric asked himself.

"Well, I just wouldn't be able to stand it," he heard his voice say with an odd little quiver. "I just wouldn't.

"Gully!" he yelled again. He began to run across the fields toward the sea. Shortly after, he began to race, feeling rather that he'd slipped a leash himself as Aunt Opal's cabin shrank into the distance behind him.

IS IT POSSIBLE that a person can live in a place all his life and not see the most obvious facts about it? Eric stood in a high field looking down at Twill's coast. He'd combed the beaches and ledges near Cantrip's searching for Gullstone, with no result. Now he had climbed up again to get a wider view, and though the point before him was one he knew well, he saw it suddenly in a whole new way.

Strangle Point. He'd always assumed the place was named for horrible deaths that had occurred there: for people choked by their nets or wedged between tidal rocks or caught in the treacherous tangle of a lampfish's mustache.

Now he realized, looking down, that it was the shape of the point that accounted for its name. A thick neck of beach shot out into the sea, but halfway along its length the ocean had made inroads. It had eroded the neck, narrowing it in one spot to some fifty yards across, before the land swelled back to its proper width. Strangle Point was itself being strangled by the sea. To Eric, this seemed more ominous than his old sense of the place, and he hung back for a minute, deciding whether to go down.

Below him, the distant forms of three sea gulls rose into the air and soared out across the water. He caught his breath. Was one Gully? A tiny sod-roofed cabin that he'd never noticed before stood in a clearing set back from the ocean. The birds had been perched there or somewhere close by, he thought. He started down the slope at once, and had not taken many steps when he saw the unmistakable figure of the old fishcatcher appear beside the cabin.

"Congratulations! Congratulations, there!" The words swept up to him on the wind, shrill and alarming and irritating all at once. They bleated in his ears, over and over, until, looking up, Eric saw that the racket was not coming from the man below at all, but from the trio of gulls he had spotted earlier. Somehow, they had circled around without his noticing. They were flying directly overhead, keeping abreast of his descent.

"Caw-qwawk! Caw-qwawk!" Congratulations indeed! What a strange mistake to make. He supposed it must come from feeling nervous about Gullstone. His imagination had leaped out and taken the upper hand. And yet, as he neared the figure waiting below, he thought he heard the words again, and others weirdly entangled in the shrieks of the gulls. This, combined with his new view of the point, seemed more than a little peculiar, and if not for Gully, Eric might well have turned around and gone home.

Zeke Cantrip raised an ordinary hand in greeting, however, when he reached the cabin.

"Ahoy, there! We thought you might blow in to-day!" The fellow looked larger than Eric remembered, perhaps because of his outfit. He was decked out in full deep-water fishing regalia: coat, hat, gloves, boots. A long black tarpaulin cape was tied over the top of everything.

"Are you expecting bad weather here this morning?" Eric asked, glancing at the sky.

"Not a bit!" roared the old man. "Just giving you a proper welcome. Your bird's over there on the roof. Perfectly fit, he is. A worn place on his foot where the rope—"

"Gully!" cried Eric, whirling around and catching sight of him. "There you are, you crazy gull!" He was nestled on the sod amid a mangy flock of wild sea gulls, looking unusually pleased with himself. But he flew down to Eric's arm the moment it was offered.

"He's been just as worried as I was," Eric said. "He's not used to spending the night out all by himself in a strange place."

"What's that?" The fishcatcher waggled an ear with his hand. "Speak up. Speak up."

"All alone in a strange place!" Eric yelled. "My sea gull!"

"He's had plenty of company, don't trouble yourself

on that score," the old man shot back. "I wonder he's not more suited to free-wandering nights with his own kind than the smoky backyard of a fisherman's hut."

"Well, he isn't," Eric declared. He was now quite sure how Gullstone had come to be here. "And I'd appreciate it if he didn't come again."

"How's that?"

"I said, leave him alone. He likes being with me!"

"What, trussed and tied like a dinner table turkey?" Zeke Cantrip's ancient eyes fixed themselves on Eric. "You can't hold down what wants to fly up, nor keep a thing back that's made to go on."

"You don't understand. I keep him safe," Eric protested.

"Safe? Hah!" The fishcatcher turned and began to hobble toward his cabin. "Come along with me," he called back. "I'll show you what's safe."

This did not seem very likely to Eric. In fact, his every sense was signaling danger. Strangle Point had a nasty reputation along the coast, and though the weather was calm at the moment, he did not trust either it or his eccentric host. Despite what he pretended, Mr. Cantrip seemed to hear and see perfectly well when he wished. Eric lowered Sir Gullstone to the ground and whispered to him fiercely,

"You stay here. No going off by yourself anymore. I'll be back in five minutes. Five minutes!"

Then he followed Mr. Cantrip toward a shack that looked, on closer inspection, as if it had been built bare-handed, by a Robinson Crusoe deprived of tools and nails. The walls bristled with driftwood and seemed more woven than constructed. The roof sprouted weeds and brambles. The chimney was a leaning tower of tin cans stuck end on end together. Why the whole house hadn't collapsed years ago or, more likely, gone up in flames, Eric didn't know.

"That chimney of yours is a fire hazard," he couldn't help telling the old man as the front door opened before him. He stepped forward bravely and marched inside.

7

I F Zeke Cantrip made a reply, Eric never heard it. Inside the cabin door, his mouth fell open. He stared at the walls and into corners of the room. He looked up at the rafters—at least he supposed the rafters were somewhere there. With everything hanging down, crowding against everything else, it was hard to tell. In some places, a person would hardly be able to walk upright.

"What is this?" he gasped. "What is all this stuff?"

Across the floor, Mr. Cantrip was lowering himself stiffly onto a homemade barrel chair and didn't immediately answer. He glanced up a moment later, though, and seeing the expression on Eric's face, smiled and raised a hand.

"My collection!" he announced, proudly. "Let me introduce you. My small collection of relics. From the beaches, you know. Over time. And a pinch of gear from the old days."

"A pinch of gear! But you've got tons of equipment

here. I don't even know what half of it's for. I've never even heard of it!"

The fishcatcher smiled.

"What is *this*, for instance?" Eric grasped a prickly looking object.

"Well, in the ancient days it hung from your belt, and when you spotted a crab far out in the current you'd throw it and—"

"And *this!*" interrupted Eric, holding forth a grisly, hairy clump of something.

"Ah, yes. A lampfish mustache. Fascinating, isn't it? I came across it one day after a storm when I was—"

"And this!"

"Well, I—"

"And *this!*"

"Yes, one day I happened to—"

"And this!"

Each thing was stranger than the last. There were shiny mirror stones and a pearl the size of a pear. There were glass water masks and deadly darts and javelins. ("Used to be more underwater work done here in the olden times," the fishcatcher explained.) There were traps of every shape, made out of every material, employing every trick ever known for catching fish and crabs. There were compasses and old maps, ships' rudders and transoms, spyglasses and shark fins, rope ladders and eel skins. The items dangled from the walls or were draped from the ceiling or piled in corners along with many, many other objects unrecognizable to Eric. Or if recognized, they looked so oddly out of context—a group of stuffed seahawks, for instance, gathering dust on a ship's wheel—or were such a strange color—everything was bathed in a rather eerie reddish light—that it was easy to confuse the ordinary with the unusual, the real with the imagined, the disgusting with the beautiful, the fragment with the whole.

In the midst of all this, Eric turned and turned, gazed and gazed, touched and drew back, until his eyes fell again on the old man. He was grinning and nodding and offering random comments from his seat:

"It's a nice collection, yes. That's a red herring, did you guess? Those false teeth were carved from a whale's jawbone. I like to remind myself how far we've come since the early days. A nice collection, I always say. Will you sit down for a minute? No need to hurry off, now that you've come such a way. Your bird's safe on my ground. We could talk of certain things. We could—"

Eric let out a cry. He had identified the source of the reddish light, and now he moved toward a glass tank half-hidden by a curtain behind the fishcatcher's seat. Its glow was so powerful that his eyes were dazzled, though only a portion of the tank was in view.

"But what is this?" he exclaimed. "What have you got here? It looks like a . . . But it couldn't be. Still, it does look exactly like the glow of a . . ."

When he hesitated again, Zeke Cantrip reached out to pull away the rest of the curtain and, with brilliant light flooding the room, supplied the word for him:

"A lampfish? Dead on course you are! I thought you might be interested. This lamp's smaller than most I've run into. I think it must've lost its grip on the current and been swept away. I found it washed up on Strangle Beach after the last storm. Are you amazed?" he asked eagerly, rubbing his hands together.

Eric was amazed. He was dumbfounded. He could not at first see the creature, because of its bright light. But in a moment, an outline appeared to him. Then the great mustaches showed themselves, swirling gently against the glass sides of the tank. He saw a pair of intelligent green eyes turn to examine him through the water. The huge pink body wallowed, then stilled, rippled, then rested. Every bone was visible, every organ and every vein. At its center throbbed the heart, steadily, monstrously, like a great bass drum beaten from within.

"How'd you ever get it here?" Eric managed to ask, after several attempts to activate his voice had failed.

"I've got a crew!" The fishcatcher winked at him. "Good workers, tried and true. Been with me for years. You saw them on the roof coming in."

"On the roof! The only thing on the roof, besides my Gullstone, that is, was a bunch of wild sea gulls!"

"That's my crew! They know how to take an order. Understand every word. Used to be, when I first moved out here by myself, I had nobody to talk to. So I'd talk to the gulls just to hear my own voice. 'Congratulations!' I'd call out, every morning getting up. 'It's a fine day for fish.' Or if the sky looked bad: 'It's a black day for fish,' I'd yell. 'D'ya think the wind'll change?'

"It got so they began to expect my talking, and they'd hang around and wait for me to start. And then, after a while, I guess they began to see what I was talking about, because I'd mention some little thing, like a trap snarled in weed, and they'd look into the problem with me. So gradually we got to working together, with them being my manpower and my crew. Of course, they don't exactly say 'Aye, aye, sir!' like a real captain gets."

The fishcatcher went into a brief laughing fit about this remark, while Eric looked worriedly over his shoulder. This was strange talk if ever he'd heard it. He remembered uneasily how the squawks of the gulls ushering him down to Strangle Point had seemed to contain words.

"I think I'll just go out for a minute and see if my bird is all right . . ." he tried to say, but the old man's hearing had taken a drastic turn for the worse. He plowed right over the top of Eric's words and proceeded to tell a story. It was a loony story, and it was told with such alarming scowls and giggles that Eric began to feel even more nervous. He edged closer to the cabin door.

"There it was, a lampfish floundering on the sand!" Zeke Cantrip was saying, though any sane person in Twickham would tell you it was impossible. Lampfish didn't flounder on dry land. "I saw it and I knew it was too big for my crew to handle. They mostly are. So I ordered my birds to call in reinforcements, and pretty soon a whole crowd of gulls turned up. Maybe your sea gull was one. Did he go off suddenly on the morning after the last storm?"

"No, he didn't," Eric replied tartly. "He was inside Aunt Opal's cabin with me."

"Well, that's too bad. It's always a big show when we take a lampfish off the beach. Gulls come from everywhere, up and down the coast."

"You've found lampfish before?"

"Sure we have. Many times. After the big storms. Strangle Beach catches them up the way it's shaped. As I was saying, when the gulls all got here, I told my crew to pass on the order to fetch my big net down to the beach, which they did. Then we tried to shove the fish onto the net. The lamps don't like that much, have their pride like anyone about being pushed around. So it thrashed pretty bad before we finally got it set. Then the birds took hold of the net and tried to fly, and after a lot of beating and flapping (I wish you could've seen it!), the net was lifted off the sand and they flew the lampfish out to deep water."

"They flew a lampfish through the air?" Eric said.

"We've got to, to help them out. The fish get quiet on the way. They can see what's happening, that we're not out to murder them like everybody else on this coast. But in the case of this one, it was injured. We all saw it right away. Something was wrong with its balance, and when it went into the water, it couldn't swim. Kept rolling over backwards.

"So we got the net around it again and flew it up here, where I have this old aquarium left over from the last century. People used to stock up on fish for the Season of Storms, you know. It was an idea that never worked very well, though. You couldn't keep 'em alive long enough to last even halfway through the season."

The fishcatcher turned and tapped softly on the aquarium's glass. Inside, the lampfish rippled and flashed forward. Eric jumped back, but a moment later the creature had withdrawn and begun to nibble a mass of seaweed near one side of the tank.

"I've been tending lampfish for a while now. Maybe the word's gone out," Mr. Cantrip said, "because they're always well behaved when they're up here with me. They know I'm trying to help. And mostly, I can. I've learned some tricks over time. What works, what doesn't. This one's got to go back in the sea tomorrow, fixed or not. You can't keep lampfish penned for long, or they get weak and die. We want to save them, but we don't want to kill them doing it. Now as I was saying about your sea gull—"

"Wait a minute!" Eric interrupted. "How could any of this be true? For one thing, the coast is crawling every day with fishcatchers fishing from their boats and casting off the ledges. If bright pink lampfish are being flown around Strangle Beach in nets by bunches of sea gulls, why has nobody ever seen it?"

The fishcatcher shrugged. "Don't ask me why people choose to see one thing and not another. I've been wondering about it for a long time myself. That's not the least of it, either. For years I've been telling people about the currents and the spouts and the lampfish around Twill. I've been talking and talking about how there's more between them than what appears, how there's another scheme at work, should anyone care to look. Which nobody does, of course. They're too busy fishing and watching the weather and going to weeps. Loony, they call me, when I try to pipe up. 'Talks in circles,' they say. 'Keep him away from the dog.' "

"That's true," said Eric, trying to hold back a grin.

Mr. Cantrip nodded. "I used to be a lampfish hunter, same as everybody in Twill. One of the best, in fact. I don't hunt them anymore, though. I try to warn them away from people. It's what my crew and I are up to most of the time these days, as if you hadn't guessed already."

"I did a little," Eric said. "You were always turning up at the worst possible moment, making the most possible noise."

"Right you are!" crowed the fishcatcher. "Do you know there's been only one lamp caught so far this year? We're proud of that. We're pleased as can be."

"But why?" asked Eric. "We need the lampfish for hooks. We've always used red bone hooks on the coast of Twill."

"Bone hooks? Fishwash! Twill is stuck in a rut with its bones. These days you can make a hook a hundred other ways. You can order steel ones by the bushel from the trading cities. Lampfish are special creatures."

The fishcatcher lowered his voice and leaned toward Eric. "They come from below."

"From where?"

"Up the spout, young fellow. Up the marvelous spout!"

Then, in another wild swing of mood, he grabbed Eric's arm and nearly crushed it with excitement.

"Have you never been out among the lampfish? Then ship with me tonight! The moon will set early, and the wind will drop. It's a perfect night to show you the sights. How the big fish rise and speak among themselves. A sort of music it is. Or a pulse or a beat. And the swirl. Oh, the swirl! Who can tell how it is. The closer you come to the spinning edge . . . the more the surge takes hold of your boat . . . the quicker the spray flies up in your face . . ."

Suddenly, Zeke Cantrip could contain himself no longer. He struggled to his feet and began an awkward stride around the room. Around and around he walked, circling clockwise, dodging the clutter at first, later tramping through it as the pace of his rounds increased.

Watching him, Eric knew he was in the grip of something strong, some ever-quickening current that moved him along. Round and round and round he went, muttering and murmuring, shaking his head from side to side. He was in the whirlpool, Eric saw. Inside his mind he was there again as certainly as when his body had been there, hurled inside the giant spout, all those years and years ago. Round and round and round before Eric's frightened eyes, and then the fishcatcher began to laugh.

8

AN HOUR later, the old man's cackle still echoed in Eric's head, though five miles lay between them by this time. Eric covered his ears. He was on Goose Wing Beach with his fishing gear spread around him. The noise rose in an even greater crescendo as a flock of sea gulls passing overhead let out a series of high mocking shrieks.

"Stop it!" Eric screamed back at them. "Scram. Get away!"

He was half-afraid they were spies. Were they members of Mr. Cantrip's band sent to track his movements? The fishcatcher was lonely. Perhaps, like many lonely people, he did not like to let go of his guests so easily. Certainly, he was a powerful talker, a man who sought to draw people near him with words. And then, after a while, he had come to believe in his own fantasies, Eric supposed. Lampfish flying through the air, flocks of gulls taking orders. Eric shivered. Back there in the cabin, he'd nearly been convinced. The creature in the tank had dazzled him. Now, outside in ordinary daylight, he wondered if a lampfish was what he'd really seen. Everything in the cabin had seemed so shifty and unreal. And the fishcatcher had looked rather too eager to impress him. And the light was poor, which is often a sign that tricks are being played.

Tricks, were they? Or spells.

Another flock of gulls flapped overhead. This time, Eric refused to look. Only Gullstone, sitting on a nearby rock, watched the group pass with attentive eyes. He was leashed again, and the string had been shortened.

"Well, what do you expect?" Eric had snapped at him. "You're completely irresponsible. You go off with anyone the moment you can, without a thought for the people who really care about you."

This was not strictly true, as Eric knew. His fright had made him exaggerate. Gullstone had been waiting patiently on the fishcatcher's roof when he'd come hurtling out the cabin door at Strangle Point. While the man hooted and howled inside, they had made their escape together up the long slope to the high fields, and then home. There Eric had gathered his traps and equipment while Gullstone stood by faithfully. But once at Goose Wing Beach—for they certainly could not go back to the ledge at Cantrip's— Eric had tied the gull up. "So I can get some work done!" he'd declared.

It was early afternoon, still time to make a decent catch, and Eric turned his mind toward fishing. The crab traps were soon baited and submerged between rocks at the swirling water's edge. Moving along the beach, Eric began casting a lightweight surf net into incoming waves, and drawing the net through the water with a practiced hand. Goose Wing was a good place for catching the plump, wing-finned fish called angel-fins by Twill's fishcatchers. In the first three casts, Eric netted two big ones.

Up the beach, other fishcatchers tossed and pulled nets in rhythms similar to Eric's. They did not try to speak or shout to one another. The surf's roar would only have drowned out their words. Singly, they labored, gaunt forms at the sea edge. As the sun descended the sky, their shadows tossed and pulled and ran in the sand behind them, growing longer and thinner than the catchers themselves, and finally fading to nothing when the sun dipped below the horizon.

The evening's first star had just appeared, and the sea water was changing from dark blue to inky black when Eric finally stowed his net in a knapsack and packed up the last of the crab traps.

"Gully? Time to go." He stroked the dozing sea gull's back. "We didn't do so badly today after all. Twenty angelfins and fifteen green crabs. Aunt Opal will be pleased. Even better, it's her turn to cook dinner!"

They had fresh angelfin filet dipped in johnnycake meal and fried golden brown for supper. And tiny wild strawberries picked by Mrs. Holly in Hurricane Hollow that morning. Aunt Opal had agreed to watch the older woman's fish lines on the ledge above Dead Man's Beach, so she'd had time to find the ripest berries. They often pooled their work this way, to the advantage of both.

"And yet, we're so different I sometimes wonder how we ever get along," Aunt Opal mused at the supper table. "Holly's all roundness and good humor, always wanting to please others and not cause an upset, whereas I am straight as an old pine tree and like to stand my ground in a rather bristly way. You'd think we'd have nothing in common, but we have. I suppose it's that we're both alone but have managed to get by. Respect is what's between us, though we may disapprove of each other's methods.

"Which reminds me," Aunt Opal went on. "Holly says Zeke Cantrip's been dead for years, so that old fishcatcher at the point can't be him."

"What?" said Eric. "How does she know?"

"Whisper and prattle." Aunt Opal shrugged. "Not my cup of tea. Holly isn't one for utterly groundless gossip, though. Her information's often reliable, in my experience. Apparently, the old fellow spent his last years in a shack on Strangle Point. He'd come to town for supplies every once in a while, as I told you. Then he stopped showing up. This was some years back. Those who knew him said he got too old to work a boat and finally drowned quite naturally one day after falling overboard."

Aunt Opal nodded approvingly. "It's the way decent fishcatchers go if they last that long. And a fitting end for us all, let me add."

"Wait a minute!" Eric exclaimed. "How do people

know for sure that he drowned? Did they find him afterward?"

"Of course not! His boat washed ashore on Goose Wing Beach. Some folks kept it a while in case there was a mistake. Then they made use of it, along with the rest of his gear. His shack's stood empty these many years. That was the last of him, all right."

Eric was disturbed by this news, but he did not allow his aunt to see it. He had not mentioned his visit that morning to Strangle Point. Now, he could not speak of how the cabin had been occupied. It was all too strange, too uncertain to talk about. After Aunt Opal had gone to bed, he sat outside in the shed yard with Gullstone, wondering what Mrs. Holly's information could mean. For if the person at Strangle Point wasn't Ezekiel Cantrip, why was he bothering to pretend that he was? And if he was, what could be the use of pretending to be dead all these years?

The more Eric thought about this, the less he trusted the old fishcatcher, with his feathery crew and uncanny knowledge of the weather. He promised himself never to set foot in the crooked little shack again. And nothing, he swore, not even the promise of seeing the lampfish, could tempt him out in the old man's boat at night.

"Keep away from that madman," he warned Gully, patting the bird's strong back. "I think he wants to add you to his flock of slaves. He knows you're a free, civilized bird and he doesn't like it. Stay with me, and you'll be all right."

He tested Gullstone's rope and stood up to go in. The moon had already left the sky, he noticed. The night was clear, just as the fishcatcher had predicted. It was quiet and windless. And deeply, densely dark. . . .

Eric was getting ready for bed when an odd ripple of longing pulsed through him. It was a wish to go out into the night. This was a stupid idea, he knew. He had to be up early to fish the next morning. There was no reason to get dressed and go back outside. He snuffed his candle and lay back on his pillow. He pressed his eyes shut, but the dark called him. Its blackness made him think of the lampfish. He imagined them rising, fiery red, from their underwater holes. He felt the breeze from their close-passing bodies, the currents made by their powerful fins. These currents pulled him along, drew him forward like wind in an alley. Am I dreaming? he wondered, and clung to his bed.

Outside, a great wind had come. Bushes scratched against the window. They were calling him, too, and he imagined getting up. Before him, the road to Strangle Point appeared, then the fields and the cliffs. He saw the ocean gleaming with lampfish. Below, on the beach, he saw the old man hunched by a boat. He was waiting to take Eric out among the fish, to show him the spout from which the creatures rose. While he waited, the wind whirled around him and clouds circled his head, as if he were the master of some invisible force and controlled more than sea gulls along Twill's cruel coast.

Eric wrenched himself away. He refused to be taken. In his mind, he turned from the fishcatcher and ran. Though the lampfishes' current seemed to drag him back, he drove his legs on and fought with his arms. In bed, he fought also, and fled beneath the blankets. At last, quite suddenly, the current gave in and cast him free. He was thrown back together, bed and mind together. Outside, the wind died. The bushes stopped beating against the window. The night became silent. He lay with thundering heart within the walls of his room. It was a dream, wasn't it? Yes, of course, a horrid dream.

ERIC HAD GONE indoors and was rustling about in his bedroom when Sir Gullstone Sea Gull first noticed the disturbance. Out in the shed yard, he stopped pecking at the string that bound him to the woodpile and turned his beak to the sky. Something was coming. His gull detection system was picking up signals: slight vibrations in the night air. His feathers quivered, but several minutes passed before he could make out the nature of what approached. He waited, straining against his bond.

He smelled the thing at last—the wild, briny stink of the open sea. Then he saw it, a pale cloud of gulls flying swiftly with the wind out of the northwest. There were a hundred birds, perhaps more. Gullstone's lemon eyes widened as the flock veered in flight and dropped toward Aunt Opal's cabin.

They passed like a massive wave within inches of

the roof, swept away, circled, and passed again. And again! Their bodies and wings shone bone white in the dark. Their formation was so dense that each sweep created a strong current of air. It caused the branches of nearby bush clumps to thrash and lift toward the sky. Straw thatches on the roof were sucked up by the draft. In the shed yard, Gullstone's feathers rose off his back. The pull was tremendous. He braced his feet to keep his body, also, from rising. And again they came. Again and again and again.

Then, as if some inaudible command had been issued, the gulls wheeled as one and ascended to a higher altitude. They spun and wove themselves into a traveling cloud once more and sped away into the night. For several minutes, Gullstone stared after them, sniffing the air in the direction of Strangle Point. Afterward, he bent his head and went to work fiercely on the string around his ankle.

Inside Aunt Opal's cabin, Eric lay in bed with wide-open eyes, and a long time passed—and many queer thoughts—before he dared to close them again.

9

ERIC woke to the ringing of bells. From the coast the clamor came, in through his window with the barely risen sun. Clang! Clang! Clang! Clang! Lampfish!

He was up in a flash, pulling on his pants, struggling with his boots. Aunt Opal was quicker after all her years of experience. He heard her run past his door before his first boot was laced.

"I'm ready!" he shouted. "I'm coming. Just wait!"

She made no reply, and why should she? Better to save her breath for the race to the coast, for the loading and unloading of nets, prods, spears, harpoons, ropes, and pulleys. And for the grueling lampfish hunt itself, yes, best above all to save breath for that.

Clang! Clang! Clang! Clang!

No breakfast today but what could be grabbed going by. No time to wash a face, button a shirt, untie a leashed sea gull. Gullstone stood miserably by the woodpile, his rope stretched to its fullest extent. His feathers were dirty, and his ankle looked raw.

"Come on!" yelled Aunt Opal. "We'll be last at this rate." She had pushed the big net onto the road and was already starting out.

"Sorry, Gully," Eric panted, rushing past. "I'll be back as soon as I can." His arms were full of ropes and prods, which made running extremely difficult. It was several minutes before he was able to catch up with his aunt on the road. But even this pace was not enough for Opal, who was in a state of high excitement.

"Faster!" she roared, as road dust billowed up in their faces. "It's Dead Man's Beach, I'm sure. The belling comes from there!"

She was right, as usual. They arrived to see Timothy Crimm swinging his ancient hand bell on the ledge above the beach. This was the very ledge from which Aunt Opal and Mrs. Holly had yesterday cast their lines. Now the scene was entirely changed. From every direction, net trolleys rumbled in, ropes and knapsacks tumbled out, and people scrambled to untangle their gear and set up the lifts.

"Where's the fish?" someone called. "Who's manning the boats?"

Timothy Crimm pointed to the wicked stretch of rocks on the southeast end of the beach. A dory hovered offshore there, riding the rocking waves. In the boat stood a young woman with an oar held straight in the air.

"Angela Hawkins saw it first," old Tim bellowed. He was always fair when it came to giving credit. "There she is, standing by. I took up the belling from her so the lamp weren't scared off. There's a crew of catchers rowing round from the harbor. Be here any moment."

"There they are!" shouted Eric. "They're here! Get the nets!"

The scrambling increased to a feverish pace at this. Two fishcatchers with forearms the size of cider kegs drove a series of metal lift pins into the ledge. Then the pulleys were threaded with ropes, the complicated lifts were rigged, and five big nets were connected to them and readied for action. Two were lowered off the ledge directly into the water; two were spread on the adjacent sand in case the big fish rushed the beach. The last was kept hidden on the lowest part of the ledge, so that it might be dropped over and snapped shut quickly should the lampfish pass under there.

All this preparation required the work of many hands. Fishcatchers of every age and description thronged the ledge and the beach, the rocks, and shallows. Everyone from town had come, it seemed, and even little-seen folk were arriving from up the coast where lampfish alarms could rarely be heard. The day had dawned quiet, and the bell had carried to distant points. And with only one lampfish caught that year, people were glad to break routine.

More than that, they were ecstatic! They whistled and shouted congratulations and shook hands and called their children over to be properly introduced.

Meanwhile, out to sea, three fast boats, each manned by a crew of three rowers, rounded the rocks off Dead Man's Beach and skimmed over the water toward the upraised oar.

"Get ready," Eric muttered to Aunt Opal. "They're almost there."

Now, the activity on the ledge and beach began to die down. All eyes turned toward Angela Hawkins, rocking up and down in her slim catcher's dory. When they had admired her proud form (and, in not a few cases, recalled themselves in her boots), those waiting on the cliffs looked down into the ocean beneath her. There, some imagined they saw a streak of red. Others swore they detected the shiftings of a massive body.

Still others saw in the curl of a wave the foamy strands of a lampfish's mustaches, though in Eric's opinion the fish was far too deep to be visible at such a distance. As the three skiffs closed on Angela, he couldn't help thinking how people often see what they hope or expect or fear most to see, instead of what is really there. And he reminded himself, rather severely, to look at things straight and hard from now on, and not to let imagination carry him away, as it seemed to have been doing recently under the weird influence of the old fishcatcher.

A cry rose from the rowers. The boats came abreast of Angela Hawkins, and in a moment six long-handled, snub-nosed prods were thrust deep in the water. These were the opening shots at the lampfish, but they were not meant to injure it. The prods were to surprise the big fish, which up to this time, if all was going well, should have been placidly grazing on seaweed without an inkling of the preparations overhead. When a fish was properly surprised, it panicked and became disoriented. Then it was more likely to swim in the direction the catchers wanted, toward shore where the big nets waited.

Seconds after the first prods entered the water, Eric saw a strong rosy back cresting the water's surface. A whoop went up from the catchers near him. The fish was smallish, but this only made the catch more likely. It dove immediately with a gush of water. Shortly, ripples appeared, showing the direction the lamp was moving.

"It's approaching the beach! Look to the beach!" several catchers shouted.

This would be an easy catch, Eric thought. The lampfish was panicked. It had surfaced in distress, and now it gave its location away by swimming a rather lopsided, shallow course. Perhaps one of the prods had struck it on the head. The creature looked oddly unbalanced.

A minute later, however, the catchers' advantage was lost when the fish regained its reason and deep-plunged. Silence engulfed the ledge. Every eye scanned the water. Beside Eric, Aunt Opal shook her head and groaned. A deep-plunging lampfish meant trouble and risk. Now the boat crews would have to attempt a far more difficult tactic. "Foiling," it was called, an archaic procedure that had been handed down for generations on Twill's coast. Its dangers were known all too well.

Offshore, the crews hastily converged their skiffs

and began to unpack the glittering foil line, which had been stowed on one boat in case of need. Old as it was—some dated the line back two hundred years— it never seemed to lose its luster. A wave of excitement went through the crowd on shore as its coils were divided and handed among the boats. Then the crews (including Angela Hawkins working heroically alone), separated and rowed to positions around the cove, letting out the line between them as they went.

The foil was next adjusted underwater from one boat to another so that it would hang at the proper depth. Correctly placed, it would act as a kind of baffle, keeping the lampfish inside the arc formed by the connected skiffs. For though the foil was thin and obviously no match for the power of a giant fish, it was strung along its length with thousands of white sharks' teeth. These sharp, gleaming objects so alarmed the lampfish that it dared not cross, though it easily might have if only the trick were known.

The danger of the method lay in the same alarm it created. Frightened lampfish were vicious fighters. It was not uncommon for a fish to attack a boat controlling the foil rope, or even, in fury, to attack the fishcatchers inside a boat. Then a whole crew might go down as friends and relatives watched helpless from shore.

These were the worst sort of deaths—anyone in Twill would testify to that. These were the sort that wormed into a person's dreams and rose up shrieking. They were the kind that could never be forgotten, because they printed so deeply on the brain. Over and over, they played before the eyes of the watchers, who were doubly helpless because they could no more save themselves from their own memories than rescue the drowning crew from the treacherous water.

So, the complicated maneuvers of the four skiffs off Dead Man's Beach were followed breathlessly by every man, woman, and child on shore. When the crews' work was completed, the foil sparkled like a fiendish pearl necklace under the cove waters. Then, the land catchers, including Eric and Aunt Opal, crept forward and readied themselves again.

Now, the rowers began the slow, time-honored advance toward the beach. If there had been drums in Twill, this is when they would have sounded, low and threatening and expectant of the kill. Steadily, the rowers rowed, prepared at every moment for attack. Stealthily, the arc of the foil was drawn closer around the prey.

At first, there was no sign of the big fish, and some on the ledge began to think it had escaped before the foil was in place, as sometimes happened. But soon the telltale red flickers appeared. Then a heave of water showed the lampfish in panic. It dove and surfaced. Dove and was still for a long minute. Eric, recalling the green eyes of the old fishcatcher's lampfish, suddenly found himself imagining the eyes of this hunted one. Wide and terror filled they would be, staring up in disbelief at the closing circle of teeth, looking around for a safe place to hide, seeing the space narrow between the cliffs and the . . .

Eric shook his head hard. Good grief, what a vision!

What was the matter with him? He made himself concentrate on the rowers' progress. They had all but cornered the fish. It was merely a matter of time before the catch was made. There! A surge of water erupted near the ledge. Eric, who was minding one of the submerged nets, leaned forward in time to see the whole fish rise and slam against the wall of rock below him. The creature appeared to have lost its sea sense entirely. Dazed, it rolled over backwards on its fins.

"Man the lifts!" Eric shouted. "It's here. Beneath!"

In an instant, ten strong fishcatchers, including Aunt Opal, sprang to the ropes and began to pull the big net up.

"Haul! Haul!" yelled the catchers around them. The pulleys shrieked. The metal lift pegs bent under the net's weight. The lifters' hands blistered and burned, but the hauling continued at top speed.

Out on the ledge, an army of catchers with more long-handled prods was in action, trying to corral the fish from above. Lower down, short-handled prods, prod hooks, spears, and grapples were out and ready, though the creature's explosive thrashings made them useless at the moment. The fish had detected the net closing around it by now, and was putting up a strong fight. Spray flew from the water, dousing the net lifters. Catchers clinging to rock niches were nearly swept away by a torrent of furious waves. In the middle of everything, five-year-old Natey Phillips slipped and fell four feet down the ledge onto the heads of a group of catchers. He was handed back up with angry yells.

And still the lift crew hauled, joined by more hands as the weight increased. Aunt Opal's face was purple with exertion. Her catcher's mackintosh streamed with salt water. Around her, everyone shouted at once.

"More prod hooks here!"

"Sam Taylor needs a spear!"

"Watch your head, Alexander!"

"The net's coming out!"

It was coming, all right, but only with enormous effort. Inch by inch, the sweating lift crew raised the net from the water. And with the net came the lampfish, thrashing, panting, scarlet with fright. Its mustaches were crushed in the weave of the net. Its body was bruised and distorted. Eric, sitting with his spear down low on the ledge, caught sight of a single green eye shining out from the ungainly mass. For a moment, it seemed to focus on him with a spark of recognition. Eric's heart jumped. Then the eye was gone, lost in another tremendous heave from the lifters above.

Soon, there was no way to tell from the twisting shape which part was head and which was tail, where a mustache began or a fin ended. At this point, the spear throwers commenced hurling with a shout. Within minutes, the net was spiked through and through, and the lampfish, though far from dead, had stopped struggling. This was a great relief to the net lifters, who were nearly at the end of their strength. They cleated their ropes and lay back gasping on the ledge. Then, before Angela Hawkins arrived to do the final honors, several tiny beginner fishcatchers were nudged forward by their parents and the charming, ages-old Ceremony of the First Blood began.

Each child clasped a shortened spear in hand and went, in turn, to the side of the ledge. There, the spear was quaveringly aimed—grown-up catchers leaned over to help—and thrown at the lampfish with every ounce of infant strength. Admittedly, this didn't amount to much, and no spear stuck very deep in the mark. Still, the children were congratulated as if they had made the kill single-handed, and their parents raised them up on their shoulders with pride. And though the littlest ones looked somewhat pale afterward (for the sight of a mortally wounded lampfish is quite shocking at first), they smiled bravely.

All this time, Angela Hawkins and the other members of the boat crews had been coiling lines, repacking the foil rope, and rowing their boats into the beach. They stepped, wet and happy, onshore, and climbed the ledge amid rousing hoorays and applause. Every one of them was a hero. The catch had gone magnificently. Angela Hawkins was the particular hero of the day, however, for sighting the fish to begin with, and then for working single-handed during the hunt. There was no question (as there sometimes was, unfortunately) that to her would go the special award, the coveted Death Strike that would finish the lampfish once and for all, and open the way for the town's victory celebrations.

She came forward to the rocks' edge, carrying her harpoon over her head so as not to run its blade into those swarming around her. The crowd hushed and fell back when she took up her position. On a small rise nearby, Aunt Opal shivered with excitement and spoke to Mrs. Holly, who had come to stand beside her.

"Such an honor!" she said. "Such a wonderful moment! I never get tired of it, though I've seen hundreds of lampfish kills in my life. I suppose it must have to do with the fright one feels going into a hunt."

"I suppose so," Mrs. Holly replied, craning her neck to get a better look.

"To be so terribly afraid, and then, to catch the great fish in the end. To come away safe and with such a prize . . . oh! It fills a person with awe and relief, and with tremendous happiness!" Aunt Opal went on. "It makes you feel that life is worth living, if you know what I mean."

This was such an unusually passionate outburst from Opal, that Mrs. Holly turned and stared at her friend. Only for the merest second, though.

"Here goes the throw," she announced a moment later, from her tiptoes. "Look at the muscles on that girl."

There was a sort of *whunking* sound, followed by a beefy gurgle and sputter, and then some gigantic thrashing noises.

"I can't quite see what's happening," Mrs. Holly remarked to Opal. "Can you?"

FROM HIS NICHE low down on the ledge, Eric's view was crystal clear. In fact, he had never known a morning in Twill to be so transparent. Never had the rocks looked so sharp or the water so desperately blue. He could see for miles in every direction. And nearby, around the ledge, he could pick out the tiniest details in the scene: a ring on a child's finger, a feather adrift in the air, a button dangling by a thread from a well-worn coat.

He saw Angela Hawkins appear, gaze over the ledge, and pucker her lips, calculating. He saw her raise her arm and sight down her harpoon shaft with a cool, squinty eye. He watched a beam of sunlight flash off the long blade. Here he glanced away. He was feeling a bit queasy for some reason. The lampfish's green eye, opening suddenly on him that way, had unnerved him. He had not even thrown his own spear, he discovered with a wave of embarrassment when he looked down. It lay upon his lap still clenched in his hands.

Luckily, no one had noticed. Everyone's attention was riveted on the lampfish, which still hung—crushed rather cruelly, it seemed to Eric, in his new clearness— inside the big net halfway up the ledge.

Angela's arm went back. Then:

Whunk!

Eric saw her harpoon drive deep into the lampfish. It was a strong throw, though a fraction off the mark. The fish flinched but was not immediately killed. Its mountainous body heaved and twisted around the terrible new shaft. A roar of appreciation went up from the throngs, though why they should be so pleased when Angela had missed her mark, Eric couldn't see.

Now the poor fish would simply hang there until it thrashed itself to death. That was the rule on the coast of Twill. And what a stupid rule it was to make the fish suffer so, Eric thought, with sudden anger.

Another sick spell passed through him. It was impossible to watch the lampfish. Why this should be when he had watched so many other kills, had cheered through them just as everyone else was doing now, he could not imagine. He turned his face away and looked off beyond the ledge, to other ledges and cliffs farther along the coast.

A mass of sea gulls had collected over the next point. It wasn't far away. He could see the group quite plainly, flying up and down, darting in and out, as if something on the ground, some morsel of food, maybe, was attracting them. He pictured Gullstone, safe at home tied to the woodpile, and thought how lucky it was that he wasn't here to see all of this.

The lampfish was beginning to die. The fishcatchers on the ledge were howling louder. They sounded like a pack of bloodthirsty wolves. Eric covered his ears. The lampfish in its final moments must believe itself to be surrounded by barbarians, by merciless killers who, now that one thought about it, might easily make their hooks from other things. Might buy them from the trading cities, as the old fishcatcher had said.

Eric's hand tightened around his spear. It was ridiculous to go on with these brutal hunts, he decided. The truth was that the hunts had become a ritual in Twill, something old to pass on to the children. Pouncing on unsuspecting lampfish. Slicing them up with wild howls. It was no different from what The Old Blaster did to the people of Twill during every Season of Storms. The Blaster preyed on Twill, and Twill preyed on the lampfish.

Eric stared along the coast. He was sick, all right, sick of drownings and killings, of wrecks and disappearings. Whatever direction you looked in Twill, they were there, waiting. Nothing could be safe, no matter what you did. Nothing could be saved. It was useless to try.

He looked around fearfully at the lampfish. He knew this fish. It was the wounded one from the fish-catcher's cabin. He hoped its green eye would not open again. . . . As he watched, the monster gave a last feeble heave, curled into itself, and lay still.

In that victorious instant, Angela Hawkins raised her fist skyward, and ecstatic cheers broke out all over the point. Then everyone was leaping up, rushing forward to help the net lifters pull the splendid fish up the ledge. What a fight he had fought! What a party the town would have that night! Aunt Opal pulled the lift rope proudly, every bit of strength restored. Mrs. Holly said she would bake a five-layer cake. Five layers! Twenty children converged on her and demanded to be taken home to help.

"All right, then, we'll make a ten-layer cake!" she cried, flinging her arms around the mob.

Low down on the ledge, Eric turned away from this appalling scene and looked out to sea. He saw the sun beating fiercely on the blue cove waters. He saw a flock of sea gulls bobbing on the swells. He saw more gulls landing on the next point down. And more, and then more. And then he raised his eyes one further inch to the electrifying profile of—

Ezekiel Cantrip! Standing like a sentry on the highest ledge! Sunlight sparked off his windblown hair. Below, his eyes were dark as two caves in a cliff.

He had seen everything, Eric was sure of it. He knew everything and stood up there to make his protest. Sea gulls swirled around his head like clouds. The sky and the sea and the rocky coast seemed to arrange themselves about him, so that he was at their center, the focus of their parts. And this was not the crude, grasping center from Eric's dream the night before, but a cooler power, older, sadder, and more persuasive by far. If he could have grown wings in that moment, Eric would have soared across to him.

"Look!" he screamed to the fishcatchers near him. "Over there. It's Mr. Cantrip. He's still alive and he knows about the lampfish. Look, he's trying to tell us! Look at him. There!"

No one paid the slightest attention. No one saw the man or his gulls. They didn't see either how the old fishcatcher raised his arms in the air as if issuing a command, and how one bird among the thousands flew down to him there, landing with a wobble on his tarpaulin shoulder.

"Gullstone!" Eric shrieked, leaping to his feet. "Gully, don't move! Wait for me! I'm coming!"

10

ISTANCES are deceptive along the coast of Twill. What appears on a clear day quite close across water may actually be several miles away. The ragged scoops and twists of coastline add miles for a person hiking between points, and thickets of thorny beach plum interrupt even these winding paths. Eric wasted no time going after Gullstone, but he arrived on the next point down to find the ledge cleared of birds, the sky empty. The crag where the fishcatcher had stood rose over his head. He climbed it at once and gazed up and down the coast.

The view was tremendous. To the south, the land swept away in open fields to Twickham, which looked minute against this backdrop, a cluster of elfin huts peeping timidly out at the sea. The north road was visible running inland, parallel to the coast. Not far along it, Eric saw the hunters from Dead Man's Beach. They were making their way to town in a triumphant parade of bobbing harpoons and prods. At the procession's end came the dead lampfish, hauled by many hands upon a float of trolleys. The sprawled body looked so pitiful, with its rosy scales gone purplish gray, that the horror of the kill cut through Eric again, and he wondered how he ever could have hunted before.

He turned his eyes north. Cantrip's Point reared up in a bristle of ledges. Beyond, the land dropped off into the steep slope that ended at Strangle Point. Just there, at the crest, he spied the old man and his swirling, flapping crew. They were headed straight back to their shack. He was down the rock in an instant, speeding off to follow. The wind veered around and came up at his back, making it easy to run across the wide fields.

"Wait for me! Wait!" he cried toward the retreating forms. And then, suddenly, not only wind, but sea gulls were at his heels. They were overhead soaring past him and flapping at his shoulders. It was so exhilarating to feel this wing power near him that his strides lengthened. His feet lost the sense of the ground, and he seemed, incredibly, to fly with the birds.

He was at the crest in a matter of minutes. Below him, Zeke Cantrip descended the slope with an old man's stiffness. Gulls flew at his elbows, supporting each lurching step. And there was Sir Gullstone, hovering gracefully among the others.

"Gully!"

The bird came at once and landed safely on Eric's arm.

"You crazy sea gull. You shouldn't be here. You never do a thing you're supposed to do!" Eric tried to look severe but was distracted by a pair of nasty gouges on one of the gull's ankles. "Oh, Gully! How could you!" He had pecked through his rope with a furious beak.

"Aha! Here you are!" cried the fishcatcher, just then turning around. Though Eric half expected lightning bolts to fly out of his hair, he appeared to be his most ordinary salty self, so much so that Eric wondered if his imagination hadn't once again gone off the track. There was not a trace of the silent, powerful figure who had stood on the crag gazing down on the hunt.

"In the nick of time, too," the fishcatcher went on. "I'm worn to the bone by this morning's wretched work. Worn fore and aft to the rib and the plank. The old ship's not fit for such jigging about. Here, lend me a hand, or this hill will be my last!"

Eric didn't hesitate this time before going down to join the man who called himself Mr. Cantrip. Whoever he was, he understood the true nature of the lampfish hunt, and that seemed quite enough for the moment. In fact, the rather shocking events of the morning had apparently worn the poor fellow out. He grasped Eric's shoulder eagerly and kept a firm grip on it all the way down. And though they hobbled toward the very shack that Eric had sworn never to enter again, he was no longer frightened by it. Nor did he mind when Gull-stone flew up to mingle again with the rowdy, ranting crew over their heads.

"Congratulations! Congratulations!" the gulls shrieked over and over, as if Eric required some special welcome.

"The lampfish that was killed was the one from your tank, wasn't it?" he asked the old man shyly, when they had walked a while together.

"Aye, it was." The fishcatcher nodded. "I'm glad you saw. Nobody else on this coast can tell one lamp from another. Me and my crew launched it early this morning, before the sun rose. We thought it'd get a safe start that way."

He shook his white head. "The fish weren't fit, like I told you before. There was nothing we could do. It was better but not fit, and it swam too close to the surface and got sighted." He sighed, and looked so thoroughly miserable that Eric's heart went out to him.

"I'm sorry," he said. "Really and truly, I am. I was sorry the whole time. I couldn't even lift my spear."

"Sorry!" the fishcatcher barked. He straightened up with a lurch. "There's no blasted use in being sorry. It's the way of things on this fearful coast. Each of us takes the risk. And the lampfish of Twill take it double the rest, for they choose to come up when they could live safe below."

"What do you mean?" Eric asked. "You've said that before. Tell me about the lampfish. What sort of creatures are they?"

"What sort! Well, let's see. Creatures like all of us that live under the gun—devilish and warmhearted, dangerous and brave, curious and cautious, nasty and afraid. If you recall that big lamp, the one you had your net out for, ready to capture like a hero single-handed? . . ." The fishcatcher coughed a bit behind his hand. "Well, it's a fine, noble fish that's been around here for years, for more years than most people have seen on this coast. But it's murdered its fair share of catchers in that time because they made the mistake of getting too close. Even lamps must look out for themselves in this place."

"I guess I was lucky you came along to stop me."

"Call it luck if you like. There are larger schemes in motion."

"Larger schemes?" Eric stopped and looked up at him. "That's what you always say. But what does it mean? Who are you anyway? My aunt says Ezekiel Cantrip died years ago. Everyone in Twill thinks your cabin is abandoned. If you're really Zeke, why are you hiding out? What's really going on out here at Strangle Point?"

Was that a smile that flickered across the old man's face? No, it was a grimace. The fellow was working desperately to get down the hill.

"What'd you say?" he croaked. "I can't hear a word over the grinding of my joints." He might have been telling the truth. Beads of sweat had formed on his forehead. His jaw was clenched in pain.

"Never mind," murmured Eric, lending his shoulder again. "I can wait a little longer to find out, I guess." Whatever schemes were in motion, one thing was clear. The fishcatcher had no special powers for making his old legs young.

HOW THE REST of that day passed Eric wasn't sure, because a warm fog enveloped the fishcatcher's shack not long after they arrived there. It felt so soft and blanketlike on his skin that a nap seemed the only reasonable response. The morning had tired him more than he'd realized. He sank down on a mound of cut meadow grass and lost sense of the time until the evening shadows began to creep across the ground.

By then, the fishcatcher had rested his legs and regained his hearty manner. He lit the wood stove in the old shack and produced from somewhere a delicious fish chowder and salt-cracker supper. (Eric kept a nervous eye on the chimney, which belched clouds of smoke and seemed ready to ignite the cabin at any moment.) They shared the food with Gully and the gull crew on the shack's front step.

"You're welcome to stay or go, as you like. But there'll be nobody waiting at home after this morning's catch, I'd guess," Mr. Cantrip said.

It was quite true. Aunt Opal and Mrs. Holly would be in Twickham that night celebrating the kill. They wouldn't miss him. Lampfish celebrations were wild affairs that often went on for two or three days. Meanwhile, no one kept particular track of anyone else. Children spent the nights together or slept out on the beaches. Their parents ate and drank and danced on the lantern-lit ledges.

"I guess I'll stay," Eric said. But immediately he felt alarmed to be away from the others. In all his life, he'd never missed a celebration before. His eye jumped to Gullstone, crouched faithfully beside him in the grass. The big gray and white sea gull looked at once so beautiful, and so dearly familiar ("We are both orphans, remember!"), that he knew his real place was wherever the gull might be. Besides, he couldn't go back to Twickham yet. The memory of the kill was too fresh in his mind.

"Tell me a little about your travels," he asked the old man on the front step, where they lingered after supper. "I'd like to take a trip myself, and sooner than I'd thought."

But Mr. Cantrip had closed his eyes, and the question dropped unanswered into the evening gloom. After a moment, Gullstone rose and stalked suspiciously around the yard. Then, perhaps feeling unsettled himself by the recent turn of events, he made a large ridiculous hop and landed like a whole feather bed in Eric's lap.

"Ooof! Gully! What's the matter with you?"

Ten minutes later, they were both gazing rather sleepily at the sky when the fishcatcher stirred beside them.

"It's a lampfish night if ever there was one!" he boomed out suddenly, making everyone jump. Several gulls on the roof above them took to the air, squawking. "A perfect night!" he went on, getting to his feet with his eyes on Eric. "And I'm taking out my boat if you care to come along.

"Loose your moorings, young fellow!" he roared, intercepting the boy's worried glance at Gullstone. "For one bent on being a traveler, you're as cautious as a cod."

There was no way to get out of going after this

challenge, though Eric's good sense sounded every alarm.

"Would it be all right if I borrowed a piece of that old net rope hanging from your rafters? . . ."

"What?" Zeke Cantrip waggled his ear. "Speak up. I can't hear."

"In your shack, that net rope. I need it for my gull."

"What?" The old man thundered. "Did you say you need soap?"

"Rope!"

"Hope?"

"Rope!"

"A wet goat?"

"Forget it," Eric muttered, while the impossible old fraud turned away with a smile. He clumped into the cabin and outfitted himself in storm weather gear from head to foot—boots, cape, gloves, and all. Giving Eric a final, triumphant glance, he tied the flaps of a decrepit oilskin hat down firmly over his ears and refused to utter another word.

11

THEY set out two hours after sunset, when every streak of light was erased from the sky.

"You stay here!" Eric told the bird, but of course that was useless. Gullstone followed them the minute their backs were turned. He flew overhead, just out of reach, and along with him went Zeke Cantrip's crew with a windy rustle of wings. Otherwise, there was no motion to the air, or to the sea either, Eric saw, as they descended the ledges. Above them, the stars glimmered feebly. Offshore, the lampfish had begun to rise. They cast rosy arcs of light up from the water, enough light for Eric to make out the beach's white sand ahead and the outline of a small dory hauled up on the shore. The sea gull crew was already there when they arrived, perched along the oars and on the wooden seats.

"Avast, you gullions! We're shoving off!" bellowed the fishcatcher, not wasting a moment. The fellow was trembling with excitement, Eric discovered when he bent over to help him push the boat off the beach. The gulls flew up with annoyed shrieks. The pair jumped in and shot out into the inky sea.

There was no question of who would work the boat. Zeke Cantrip was into position in a second. Eric saw that for all his awkward lurching on land, at sea he was a master of precision and grace. The oars flashed like two batons in his hands. The dory cut cleanly through the waves. He could turn the boat with a flick of one wrist. He could spin and loop, glide and weave. And when, approaching a dangerous channel between two rocks, he lay one oar aside and proceeded to scull with the other from the stern, Eric was astonished at the speed he achieved. No current could touch him at such a pace. No reef could rear up that he couldn't slip past. He had twice the skill of the best rowers in Twill.

"Away, you birds. Mark us the spout!" Zeke Cantrip called to his crew, which flew in the darkness over their heads. So the gulls circled away, and not long after, Eric saw them hovering in a dim cloud in front of them.

"There it is!" shouted Zeke above the wash of his sculling. "Keep your eye sharp on it, and we'll not be surprised."

"Is Gully with your birds?" Eric cried. "I can't see where he's gone!"

"He's there. He's there. You've no cause to worry."

But Eric did worry. He didn't like to think of Gullstone flying near the whirlpool. Who knew what evil winds lurked over the place, or what sudden paws of spray might reach up to slap him down. Already the dory was in the grip of some current. Small waves snapped at the bow. The water raced beneath.

The fishcatcher was not bothering to scull so hard. His oar was no longer necessary to keep the boat in motion. More and more, he held it still and used it as a rudder. They were being carried in a large circle clockwise around the gulls, Eric saw, and at such a speed that wind ruffled his hair on this otherwise perfectly windless night.

"Ha, ha! We're in it now! There's the surge that stirs the blood. Hold on tight, and we'll steer a bit closer!"

"Closer!" cried Eric. "I think we're near enough!"

The gulls were not more than fifty yards from them by now. Though the water the boat circled was smooth, it was rounded at its center in a most unnatural way, like the water that spun above the Twickham street drains as they emptied the gutters after a heavy rain. This sight was so frightening to Eric that he forgot to notice why he could see it at all. The fishcatcher pointed and gestured toward the spout.

"Lampfish!" he crowed. "Coming in from all over! Look there, and there. Here's one at our stern!"

Suddenly the big fish were everywhere around them. The glow from their enormous bodies illuminated the sea in all directions, and the dory itself was bathed in rosy light. Eric saw Zeke Cantrip's face take on a rich red color as he leaned over the water to admire the creature floating there. He saw the skin on his own hands flame up as another fish rose in their path. And then, there was something else—a noise.

At first, it seemed to be the whir of their boat coursing through the sea. They were moving around together in the whirlpool's current—dory, lampfish,

water, and wave. But soon the whir became a drone, and the drone became a hum whose pitch climbed steadily in Eric's ear.

The fishcatcher waved to catch his attention. "Don't look so white. It's the lampfish," he yelled. "They mourn tonight. They sing for the lost one."

"Why are they here?" Eric screamed back. If he'd dared to let go of the dory's side, he would have covered his ears. The singing vibrated painfully in his head.

"To greet the new fish from below. You'll see it come in a moment or two. The spout reverses and sends it up."

"What?" yelled Eric. He couldn't believe his ears.

Zeke Cantrip laughed at this, and tapped his own ears, knowingly. Then he held up his hand. "Wait!" he howled. "Anytime now. Soon!"

He was perfectly right. Not more than five minutes later, the whirlpool's current began to slow. Then it ceased entirely and the dory was released from its grip and began to drift in a more or less aimless pattern. The lampfish near them drifted also, and their humming died away, though they glowed more vividly than ever. Eric took a deep breath and leaned back against the bow.

"It's the moon that does it," the fishcatcher said. His voice echoed over the water, so silent and calm had the ocean now become. "Or rather, it's her being away."

"The moon?"

"So it is on the coast of Twill. And always has been

from who knows what beginning. Have you never seen it? The moon holds sway over the tides and the spouts. And she keeps a tight grasp on them most of the time. But there's one or two nights during a month when she's sunk out of sight, and briefly far enough off to give the elements free play. That's when the lampfish dare to come."

"From where?" asked Eric.

The fishcatcher's eyes gleamed. "From beneath, like I say. From Underwhirl, as I call it, though it has more ancient names. Look there."

Eric looked at the flat ocean around them, turned deep red now by the glowing lampfish, and saw a bubble of current. A small spout of water leaped up from the sea not twenty yards off. It rose higher, and thickened, went higher, and gushed, a pillar of water so large that the spray from it splashed upon the fishcatcher's dory and doused them thoroughly in their seats.

Then, at its base, Eric caught sight of a lampfish rising out of the sea. It was shot up into the water spout and sent out to drop neatly into the sea not far from their boat. At this, the other lampfish converged on the newcomer. The piercing hum began again, and the great mass of fish boiled and thrashed like a fiery caldron, and drifted away from them. The ocean darkened under their boat.

Eric let out his breath. Already the water spout had begun to subside. Though it rose more weakly, it was fascinating to watch. The dark silver gush, now lit only by stars, poured down in a glimmering veil upon the surface of the sea. And this was no strange sea, but Eric's own, the sea he looked out on day after day, night after night, the sea that all of Twill lived with and fought with and believed it understood.

Away in the dark, Twill's craggy coast appeared only as a dim line upon the dark horizon. A few lights sparkled here and there. Otherwise, there was no sign of the town of Twickham, or the outlying houses, or the many lives being lived under the thatched and rethatched roofs. "Larger schemes," the fishcatcher had said, and here they certainly were, for this night sea was as remote from Twill as Twill was from it. No one onshore had the least idea of what was happening out here; of what had been happening, Eric thought suddenly, for hundreds, no, probably thousands of years.

"Why do they come?" he asked the old man, who sat awestruck himself beside Eric in the dory. "The lampfish, I mean."

Zeke Cantrip turned with a mischievous grin. "Why, to live!" he exclaimed. His chest heaved suddenly, and a giggle burst from his lips. "It's hilarious!" he crowed. "They come up to live, when every fish knows what the end must be. To be hunted and hunted and hunted and caught. Hysterical!" he screamed, bending over to hold his side. "Insane!" he shrieked, while Eric shrank against the bow. "Madness, looniness, dementia, death!" He dissolved into helpless giggles.

The spout had disappeared back into the ocean waters by this time. Eric sensed the rippling of new currents under the dory. Overhead, the sea gull crew reformed and marked a spot not ten yards off. Eric thought he saw Sir Gullstone circling with the others, but without the glow from the lampfish all was dark again and he could not be sure.

"Mr. Cantrip!" Eric called. He reached out to grab the shaking shoulders. "Zeke! The whirlpool's reversed again. Look! We're starting to move."

His words made no impression on the poor man. He was caught in another of his horrible fits and could no more guide a boat than a baby at sea. Meanwhile, the current was picking up. Eric heard the slap of waves under the dory's bow. With a quick movement, he slipped past the fishcatcher and grabbed the oar that still hung from the stern.

He began to scull. Though he didn't have a tenth of Zeke Cantrip's skill or strength, the boat started to move away from the spout's center. Slowly, in ever-widening circles, Eric sculled. He kept an eye on his mad companion, jumping up when necessary to haul him back into the middle of the boat. The fellow was in danger of laughing himself over the side and into the soup.

It was now, of all worst possible moments, that Gullstone chose to appear. Perhaps he'd been watching Eric's struggle from the air. With an awkward flap, he landed on the bow just behind the fishcatcher, and looked anxiously at his friend.

"Gully! Watch out! You'll end up in the water!" Eric cried. The bird was big and his perch unsteady. The dory plunged and rose on the waves. He staggered, flapped his wings, caught himself, and lifted away. But immediately he tried to land again.

"No, Gully. Get away from here! Fly with the others."

The sea gull seemed determined to stay. He moved to a place further inside the boat, spreading his wings for balance whenever the boat rocked hard. The current under them had become strong. Eric was still making headway, but he needed all his concentration to guide the boat. His sculling arm had begun to ache.

He was looking back at the whirlpool's black surge when Zeke Cantrip sprang up and placed one precarious boot on the gunnel. The dory lurched and listed in the water. Gullstone lost his perch and flapped rapidly. Eric whirled around, but it was already too late. The fishcatcher was on his way into the sea, knocked over by the sea gull's powerful wings. They had become entangled in his cape. With a half-strangled cry, the gull was pulled into the water on top of Zeke Cantrip. Eric threw down his oar and tried to grab them. But the surge whisked them beyond his reach. He held out the oar to the old man.

"Take hold. Take it!" Beyond, Gully was being swamped by the cape. It had wrapped around his body and now threatened to drag him under. He squawked and flapped desperately.

"Grab the oar!" Eric yelled, again. To his relief, the old man did, and for a few seconds they were carried together by the current. Round they went in the cold black stream, boat and oar, fishcatcher, and gull. And though the situation was extremely dangerous, Eric still hoped they might save themselves.

"I'm pulling you in!" he shouted to Zeke. "Keep a tight hold." He didn't see the grin that flicked across the briny face.

"Ahoy!" shouted the madman. "I'm pulling *you* in!" Before Eric could help himself, he was yanked into the water. The dory rebounded away, and he was swept into the whirlpool's treacherous current.

12

ERIC'S first thought was that the water was icy, and that he must kick off his boots, which were beginning to drag him down. When he had managed to free himself, he looked around for Gully. Or rather, since he swirled in utter blackness, he listened, and heard somewhere off to his left the sound of struggling. He struck out, swimming with the current in that direction. Not far away, he ran into a glove drifting just beneath the water's surface, and then another piece of clothing, which seemed to be a hat.

Ahead, the struggling noises continued, but some minutes passed before he was able to catch up. At last, he made out dimly, by starlight, the thrashing form of the fishcatcher, who was trying to rid himself of his cape.

"Your gull's gone under!" he cried when Eric reached them. "He's dragging me down! We're wrapped up together in this dratted piece of tarp!"

Immediately Eric dove, and feeling a lump of sodden feathers below the old man's churning feet, he hauled it up with all his strength. By sheer luck, Gull-stone's head rose clear and uppermost from the water. Eric was able to untwist the heavy cloth from the gull's body while keeping his bill above the surface. This loosened the garment's hold on Zeke Cantrip, as well, and shortly he flung the cape away.

His mania had passed in the furor of the moment, and been replaced by a strangely buoyant good humor. He thanked Eric for coming to his rescue and com-plimented him on his excellent swimming. And though he looked worried when Gullstone choked and spat up seawater, he appeared generally unconcerned about the danger they were in. Rather, he seemed to relish the situation.

"Glad you decided to join me!" he shouted as they coursed along together with the current. Apparently he'd forgotten pulling Eric into the water. "So pleased to have you here! What a night for it, eh? Not a cloud in the sky."

To Eric, this was madness of a different order and, in its way, more unsettling than a fit of laughter. He tried to paddle away from the wretched man. But the insistent flow moved them always together and also foiled every attempt to swim from its grip.

"We're lost," Eric gasped to Gullstone, after some frantic kicking had proved completely useless. "There's no hope of getting free. Why I ever agreed to come out here at night, I don't know. It's my fault, Gully. And now you're caught, too."

He tried to lift the gull up where he might flap a bit and shed enough water to launch himself into the air. But the great bird was exhausted from his battle with the cape. He could barely raise his head, let alone two sodden wings. Eric clung to him to keep him from sinking again.

"Never say you're lost!" the fishcatcher's voice boomed cheerfully beside them. "You're never lost till you're lost, and that you never know. As for us, there's a lampfish coming up on our starboard bow."

Eric floundered around to what he thought might be his right-hand side. An eerie red glow was seeping up through the water. Just then, however, Sir Gullstone went limp. Perhaps the cold had undone him, or exhaustion, or a wrong gulp of water had lodged in his lungs. His head flopped over into the sea, and the weight of his body seemed to double. Eric's heart jumped with fear.

"Wake up, Gullstone! You can't die now." He shook the bird wildly. "Open your eyes! Don't give up. Oh, please don't give up."

Beside them, the lampfish surfaced like a small mountain and cruised to within a dozen yards, as if to investigate the cause of their struggling. It moved easily through the current, trailing foaming streams of mustache and carrying its luminous body high in the water so that light poured unobstructed into the night and across the sea. Eric was blinded, and so frightened that he stopped shaking Gullstone and cowered in the water. But soon the current spun him along, and since the creature made no move to follow but continued to wallow in place, flashing its pale green eyes, he dared to breathe again. He cradled Gully in his arms and persuaded himself that warmth still came from the bird's body.

The fishcatcher had drifted away from them, Eric noticed in the blaze of light. He lay on his back some ten yards off, looking up at the sky. Perhaps he was hoping his gull crew would appear.

Eric followed his gaze, and for a moment, it seemed possible that help might come from this quarter. He remembered the story of how the gulls had lifted lampfish off the beaches in nets. But then his eyes came back to the rosy-lit sea, and Eric saw how foolish even this meager hope was. For though in the dark it had seemed that they were being swept along the surface of the ocean, the lampfish's light now revealed that they swam upon a vast, sloping wall of water. Whether they had passed unknowing over the whirlpool's lip, or the ocean had simply been sucked away beneath them, there was no telling. They were inside the immense bowl of the spout. Above and below them the sea revolved. The motion was slow, almost lazy in the upper reaches where they presently drifted. But as the funnel narrowed lower down, the tilting, watery wall increased its speed.

Looking around, Eric guessed that he and Gullstone were only about a third of the way down the whirlpool. Each round they made sent them noticeably lower, however. Far below, he watched the funnel's sides spin closer and closer, and finally slurp together. There was no gnashing of waves or flying spray, no alarming roar of surf. Somehow, this simple, final slurp was more frightening than any violence. Methodical and precise the whirling water seemed, as if, after endless centuries of destruction, the spout no longer bothered with theatrical ragings and foamings, but prepared for its kill with a deadly indifference.

Eric hardly breathed as he thought these thoughts and took in the terrifying view. He hugged Gully's poor, wet body closer. It was no drag on him now. He was pinned, weightless, to the spout's whirling side. No amount of swimming or thrashing would have changed his course an inch. Ahead, the lampfish floated, a fiendish torch. Of Ezekiel Cantrip there was no sign. Once, glancing up, Eric saw what appeared to be a distant flock of birds hovering against the fast-shrinking circle of the sky above. But, by then, rescue was far beyond question. A little later, he thought he heard an echo of riotous laughter. The water's incessant circling had made him dizzy, though, and he could no longer be sure of what he saw or heard.

They began to spin more rapidly still. The whirlpool's pit drew steadily closer. Eric shuddered and closed his eyes. Above the monotonous noise of rushing currents, he caught the sound of a rather ordinary gurgle. It reminded him of emptying sink drains he'd heard in his life, and he knew he had only a short time left.

He began to whisper hurried good-byes to Aunt Opal and Mrs. Holly, and to his friends at school. He bade farewell to his dead parents—he wished he could remember them better—and to Twill itself, though his existence there had not been happy.

When he finished, he buried his face in Gully's wing and tried to wait bravely for the end. There was nothing to get upset about, really. A quick turn, a tiny slurp, and the thing would be done. A person might even feel a little disappointed at the idea of being polished off so easily. Especially when everything you'd heard about whirlpools had led you to believe that going down into one would at the least be exciting, in a desperate, struggling, bone-crunching way. One slurp? How pathetic. One tiny swallow? How unfair! How degrading and infuriating, actually. How . . . !

Eric was clenching his fists underwater and beginning to fight the current again when a flash of light exploded in his face and he was engulfed in a fiery mass. He was so terrified that his arms flew apart and he dropped Gullstone with a shriek. Then all that had been around him fell away, and a black, breathless space opened up.

So this, he thought, is how it feels to meet one's end. An odd slithery-ghostly sensation. A certain rising. And floating.

So this is how . . . Eric's heart stopped pounding. He wondered vaguely if it was beating at all. Everything felt so unreal. It would be easy to mistake the scene, to think oneself dreaming or drugged or in the grasp of a powerful book. He called out to Gullstone in case the bird, wherever he was, hadn't got the idea: "All right, Gully! Don't worry, it's over! We are now thoroughly and completely killed!"

So this was how it was to be dead, yes, dead. They were done for and done in, yes, yes, yes. They were finished, wiped out, washed up, bumped off, passed on, shot down, belly up dead.

Eric's last words were, "Gully, I know you can't believe this but, guess what? We really are . . ."

13

"OPEN your eyes, young fellow. You're missing the sights," said a voice in his ear.

Eric's eyes snapped open.

"No use being a traveler if you don't take a look at where you've come."

It was the fishcatcher. He was lounging, soaking wet, against a large moss-covered boulder. In his lap sat Sir Gullstone, wildly tousled. Whole clumps of feathers had been broken off or bent in half. His wings were soggy gray, and water dripped from his bill. But there was an outraged look in his lemon-colored eyes that Eric knew from their earliest days. The bird was all right. The tough old thing had survived yet again.

"Oh, Gully!"

The old man spoke testily. "There's no need to stand there gurgling over his condition. I did my best to keep him together under the circumstances. You look like a double-drowned guttersnipe yourself. And where are your boots? You didn't go and kick them off up there, did you?"

Eric opened his mouth. He was unable to speak. He was so surprised to be alive, and so thankful that Gullstone had been saved, and so pleased, in spite of himself, to be back with the fishcatcher again, that he could only stare.

"Didn't I yell to keep 'em on? I suppose you'll say you didn't hear in all that ruckus and commotion. You could've used them down here. Never mind. We'll think of something."

Eric reached out to touch Gullstone gently. "You crazy bird. I thought you were dead."

"You mean you thought *you* were dead," Mr. Cantrip declared. "I've never seen such a wilted flower act as the one you put on coming down. I've been yelling and yelling for you to open your eyes. You missed the Underwhirl lampfish, you know. Hundreds of them came up to fetch us. They lit our way brilliantly during the whole passage down. It's a big event for them when visitors make the drop from the upper world."

"I was sure we were killed," Eric replied. "I remember seeing a great fiery light. And then . . ."

He closed his eyes again and sighed. He was feeling so sleepy and happy. Every bit of fear had been swept away. He sat down beside the fishcatcher and stretched his bare feet out luxuriously. The air had the lazy warmth of a summer day. The ground felt as soft as a carpet. After the mad swirl and pull of the whirlpool, the quiet here was like the sudden calm in Twill that came sometimes at the end of a storm. To Eric, it was deeply soothing.

"Can we stay here?" he murmured. "I don't feel like moving for about the next three years."

"Well, you've certainly picked up the spirit of the place," the old man said, squinting at him. "Most people take a little longer to put their roots down."

"Is this really Underwhirl?"

"It is." Mr. Cantrip looked around with satisfaction. "And completely unchanged from my last visit here. I'd begun to doubt it, you know. Time passes up above. A person gets old. And forgetful. 'Did that really happen to me all those many years ago?' you ask yourself. 'Did I dream it or read about it in a book?' There are some things you like to be sure of before the end. I decided to take a chance and come for a second look. Trusting in the lampfish, you understand. After all I've done for them, I was hoping they'd see me through. Not everybody makes the journey in one piece, as you've probably figured out already."

He turned and glanced at Eric. "And speaking of that, I hope you won't hold your trip down here against me. It's lonely traveling single, and you kept announcing how you were ready to go. Of course, at the time I couldn't give you the exact details of departure and arrival and mode of transport because—"

"Because I never would have come!" Eric angrily finished for him. "That goes without saying. I never would have come within a hundred miles of that creepy shack of yours, or of Strangle Point, if I'd known. And neither would Gully. Especially not Gully!"

There were a few minutes of rather strained silence after this, during which Eric stared at the sky and thought what a terrible risk they had run, and of the needless dangers they had just barely survived. Meanwhile, the fishcatcher ran his fingers through his damp, white beard, and looked uncomfortable.

"So this is where you came before when you went down the spout," Eric said at last. He was quite angry still. "Why didn't you ever tell anyone? People in Twill would be interested. It's peaceful here."

The old man looked relieved that Eric had spoken. He shook his head and raised pleading shoulders.

"I tried!" he protested. "Didn't I say I tried? They couldn't hear me. Absolutely could not hear. People have ideas of their own in a place like Twill, cast-iron ways of thinking that cannot be changed. For them, there's no hearing or seeing what doesn't fit the known order of things."

"But this is real!" Eric exclaimed. "You should have told them it was real. I can see it myself, and it's really here."

He gazed about at the tranquil landscape, so different in every aspect from Twill's rugged coast. Here sparkling fields rolled away from them in easy folds toward a horizon that promised more of the same. Here, everything was green and seemed to bask in a golden light, though no sun actually appeared in the sky. A number of large, pink clouds drifted lazily over their heads. Eric kept expecting to feel a fresh breeze against his cheek, as he did in Twill when the weather was clear. But the air remained still despite the movement above.

"I suppose next you're going to tell me that's the reason everybody in Twill thought you were dead all those years," Eric said to Zeke. "They couldn't see what you were talking about, and after a while, they couldn't see you."

"Right you are!" cried the fishcatcher, with a grin that Eric didn't particularly trust. "That's exactly what happened. After they found my boat, which had got loose one night, there wasn't any persuading them that I wasn't drowned. Of course, I wasn't going into town much anymore, being so disgusted with the way people yelled and ran off. To be truthful, I didn't care what they thought by then."

Gullstone climbed over onto Eric's lap at this moment and started a strenuous bout of grooming. He pecked and pulled his back feathers, and smoothed down his tail feathers, and combed and recombed (with his bill) the downy parts of his stomach and breast. Then, with a burst of flapping he tried to fly up, but Eric held him fast.

"You can let go of your bird," the fishcatcher said, nodding. "He's not going anywhere down here. It'll be a wonder, in fact, if he can get off the ground."

Eric rose to his feet and set Gullstone down among some clumps of grass. Then he watched nervously as the bird strutted away several yards. After all they had been through together, he felt more protective than ever and did not want to let the gull out of his sight for a minute. Nor did he, in this crucial matter, like to rely on the advice of Mr. Ezekiel Cantrip, who had tricked and alarmed him so many times. The fellow was completely unpredictable. Who could be sure, even now, that they weren't under the influence of some ridiculous spell? Eric scooped Sir Gullstone off the ground and walked back toward the boulder.

"Mr. Cantrip," he began.

The old man raised a hand. "I know, I know. You want an accounting of this place. You're a traveler at heart, I can see. Not content to pass through with a glance and blink. Got to have the details of what's under what. Well, I've done some research, let me say, since I dropped down here by accident all those years ago. What with my own travels since, I've put things together. I've seen some, though not all, of the larger design. If you'll leave that poor gull alone for a minute and come sit down, I'll give you the story. That's right, put him down. No, don't worry—he'll stick near."

Then, though Eric wasn't at all sure he was the sort of traveler the fishcatcher had in mind or that he should believe what he was about to hear, the fishcatcher began to tell the history of Underwhirl: how it was the first, the most ancient, and the most beautiful world of Earth, the core from which their own present world had evolved; how this original core had been enveloped by oceans, submerged by time, left behind as newer worlds rose and became peopled and were built over it. So for eons it had lain, deep and unchanged, below the surface. And though all signs of it had vanished, it remained connected to the upper world by means of a series of whirlpools that had sprung up through the oceans in earliest times.

"In former days, the old world beneath the whirlpools was not forgotten," the fishcatcher explained. "It was part of our world's history, and the whirlpools' connections were understood. Later, the whirlpools shriveled and became fewer, and people began to forget, not only in Twill, but everywhere. Now there are fewer spouts still, and those handful are often found in out-of-the-way places, where our upper world's habit of change hasn't so fiercely caught hold."

"And the lampfish?" asked Eric. "What part do they play?"

"But they are exactly what they are called," Zeke Cantrip replied. "Lamp fish. The name is ancient. They are and always were the guides and lights to Underwhirl. They come and go between the worlds. I suppose in the deep past there were many more of them, and that when people on our shores looked out upon their rosy lights, they were reminded of the vast, unchangeable world below. Perhaps they were comforted to know that it would be there forever. The upper world has always been a place of such furious change. Not that it shouldn't be, of course. That's the way of life. I've always been in favor of moving on and out, of not holding things back, as you know very well."

He looked pointedly at Eric, who sent Gullstone a guilty look.

"The strange part," the fishcatcher continued, "is that the name of the lampfish should be so well remembered in Twill when its real meaning was lost long ago."

"It's even stranger how Twill got fixed on the lampfishes' red bones, and a whole different idea of the great fish grew up," Eric added. "Why didn't you tell me any of this before? I would have stopped hunting the minute I knew."

The fishcatcher shook his head and laughed. "Ha!" he replied. "You'd never have heard me. You were as deaf as the rest till I got you down here."

Eric thought this unfair since in his view he'd listened quite hard to Zeke Cantrip, when he wasn't giggling and blathering on about nothing. There was no time to protest, however. Suddenly the old man was up on his feet, gesturing at the horizon with his usual melodrama.

"Speaking of moving on!" he bellowed. "It's time to hoist our sails."

"Is there a storm?" Eric cried in alarm. He jumped up and made a grab for Gullstone.

"A storm! That's a good one! Don't you know there's never been a storm in Underwhirl? And never will be, neither, just like there'll never be a sunset or a moonrise or a hot day or a cold one. Nothing moves down here, in case you hadn't noticed. Nothing changes or moves. It's always the same." Mr. Cantrip started to lurch away.

"Wait!" shouted Eric. "That's not true at all. What about those big pink clouds floating over our heads. What about . . ." He looked around for other examples.

"What about . . ." There wasn't anything he could see at the moment. No wind, no wisp of fog or bird going by.

"What about those big, rose-colored clouds?" he

yelled again, for lack of other evidence. They were most certainly moving across the sky.

Up ahead, the old man came to a halt and turned around.

"Suit yourself," he called back, with a touch of impatience. "But nothing moves nor has moved since before the dawn of time. Except the lampfish, of course." He waved his hands toward the clouds.

"Lampfish!" Eric looked up.

He saw them immediately: enormous pink-scaled fish trailing streams of foamy mustaches across Underwhirl's bright sky.

"Ho!" cried Mr. Cantrip. "You never expected to see them there, did you? And so you didn't. There's the mind of Twill at work. You'd best be rid of it down here."

"Lampfish," Eric murmured, staring up in awe. He had never seen them in broad daylight before. They were drifting about with the same magical glow as when they swam in the waters off Twill's coast. But here they swam unafraid, in the open, as if air rather than water was their natural element, as if they didn't have a single worry in the world.

And they didn't! Eric realized suddenly. He stood gazing up, clutching Gullstone in both arms. Or rather, they wouldn't if they never went up the whirlpool. If they stayed here forever where no one could hunt them, where no storm could touch them and there was no need to hide.

"Mr. Cantrip!" The fishcatcher had already put quite a distance between them, Eric saw with a start.

"Wait, wait! Don't leave us behind!" He wrapped Gullstone tightly against his chest and raced to catch up.

"Why are we always racing to catch up with Zeke Cantrip?" he muttered to the bird as they panted down the road. "There is something about him that pulls us along. In Twill, in Underwhirl, it doesn't matter where we are. Willing or unwilling, we follow either way!"

Gully lay his head sympathetically against his friend's shoulder.

14

EVER had Eric felt as happy as he now began to feel, walking with the fishcatcher through Underwhirl's lands. Never had he felt so pleased to be in a place. The comparison with Twill was breathtaking, for in almost every detail, Underwhirl was different. Where Twill was rough and spare and sparse, Underwhirl poured forth every kind of natural luxury. Fields of flowers, for instance, soft grass, blossoming trees. The road they traveled was smooth and warm under his bare feet, and so flat that Eric wished he had his trolley to race along it. There were no cliffs or ledges, no cowering huts or toppled-down barns.

There was no ocean anywhere in sight and, along with this, no anxious glance for the threatening thundercloud. There was no scanning the horizon or raising a finger to the wind. There was no wind! That took care of that. There was no sun either, apparently. But a sparkling transparency lay over the view, as if everything were encased in high-polished glass.

It was not long before Eric took the fishcatcher's
advice and put Gullstone on the ground to fend for
himself. The bird had quickly become too heavy to
carry, and there was no danger that Eric could see.
Also, though he didn't like to complain, his unshod
feet had begun to wear. A blister had already formed
on the bottom of one heel, causing him to limp.

"Aha!" the old man cried when he saw the trouble.
"I was afraid of that! Hold on a minute, and I'll have
you fixed up." He sat down at once by the roadside
and took off his boots and his heavy fishing socks.
Reaching inside a boot, he removed its leather sole
lining. This he fitted inside one of the socks, making
an ingenious slipper shoe.

"Quit worrying about that gull and jump yourself
into these," he said, when he had finished the second
sock. "You'll be glad of them by the end of our road."

"Are you sure Gully will stay with us?" Eric asked,
after he had put on the socks gratefully. "I wouldn't
want him to get lost down here."

Zeke Cantrip rolled exasperated eyes. "And where
would the beleaguered bird go? Not up, that's certain."

It was perfectly true. Gullstone could not fly. He
trooped along behind them in a sort of flapping canter.
Every once in a while he would spread his wings and
lunge upward. But two or three feet was the highest
he could go before falling back in a jumble of wings.

Eric was rather relieved when he saw this. Flying
was such a dangerous business. In Twill, he had never
liked the way Gullstone could disappear for hours at a
time. How much better that Underwhirl did not allow

it, he thought, though Gully looked a little frustrated. The poor bird could not seem to understand the new rule and kept beating his wings in furious attempts to rise.

And then, as they walked, Eric began to feel heaviness in his own body. His arms and legs acquired weight. His shoulders stooped beneath an unseen burden. The fishcatcher felt it, too. He walked slower and slower and finally called a halt to rest. But he was nervous about stopping for too long and urged Eric to his feet after only a few minutes.

"Where are we going, and how much further is it, if you don't mind my asking," Eric demanded, when they halted a second time, more tired than ever. "We could use a longer rest after that struggle in the spout. Do we need to be in such a rush?"

"We're going to the settlement on Underwhirl's lower flank. But there's no rush about it," the old man replied, giving Eric a quizzical look. "We have all the time in the world, and more."

"Then why—"

"Because we've got to keep moving! Come on. Let's go."

"Wait a minute! That was less of a stop than we made before! Gully looks as if he's on his last legs."

"And that's exactly the reason why we must move along!" cried the fishcatcher. "Now, up, up, or we'll be moored here forever."

So they plunged off again across the very beautiful and very still countryside of Underwhirl. It wasn't that they were hot. The day was a most perfect temperature.

Nor were they thirsty or hungry. Eric had never felt better in his life. The trouble came when he walked, or moved forward in any way. Then it seemed that the air refused to part, that the road wrestled with his feet and the landscape itself conspired to hold him in place with the charming stillness of its views.

"Stop! Stay!" everything commanded. "Why go any further when you have all of this!"

Nevertheless, Eric fought ahead. He was curious about what the settlement might be. Not once along their route had he caught sight of another person or any signs of human life. For that matter, he had seen no animals, insects, or birds. A rather unusual place Underwhirl was turning out to be, but whatever he might find, nothing could take away Eric's pleasure at being here. Safe was how he felt, for the first time in his life. Or rather, safe was how he was beginning to feel, how he saw it might be possible to feel if only he could stay in the place long enough.

"No storms!" he could be heard muttering incredulously to himself as they plodded along. "No tides or currents! No weeps! No fishing and"—here he glanced over his shoulder, just in case—"no Old Blaster!"

And he was most pleased of all to see his great lovable bird flapping along by his side like a well-trained dog, even if the gull did look a bit ragged from the effort. Even if his fine, white wings dragged for whole minutes on the ground now, and his arrogant head was bent, and there was a wobble in his walk that Eric hadn't seen before.

. . .

THEY HAD HALTED and gone on, halted and marched ahead so many times in the last however many hours it was ("No use counting time," Mr. Cantrip observed. "It ran out here long ago, if there ever was any"), that Eric didn't bother to glance around when yet another halt was called on yet another radiant hillside. But his eye leaped up a minute later at the sound of the fishcatcher's voice.

"There it is!" the old man wheezed. "Look, the settlement. At last!" The trek had exhausted him. He leaned forward and put his hands on his knees to catch his breath.

"Where?" asked Eric. Despite the distance they had traveled, they were standing in a place so like the one they had started from, that a person might easily have mistaken the two.

The fishcatcher had sighted something new, though. "There!" he cried, with a weary gesture. He began to limp toward an ancient and disreputable grove of trees. Eric followed, and though he peered and squinted and tried to rid himself of the mind of Twill, as the fishcatcher had advised, the grove refused to look any way other than ordinary. However, as they drew closer, a general rattle of branches arose, and a few less gnarled and twisted forms seemed to lean toward them.

"Ahoy! Ahoy, there!" the fishcatcher cried in a delighted voice. And to Eric: "Come ahead, young fellow. We've made it, I think!" Then again: "Ahoy!" to which there came a collective rustling reply that might have been "Ahoy!" or some more foreign greeting.

And then they were among their welcomers, who were not trees at all, Eric finally saw, but people standing, sitting, and stooping among trees, people woven among trees in such a way that Eric could not see clearly which was tree and which was person. His confusion was increased by the rootedness of the figures. They looked as planted in the ground as the trees themselves, and, on closer inspection, appeared to have only the vaguest suggestion of legs.

Zeke Cantrip was not worried by any of this. He was in the middle of a jubilant reunion, hobbling to and fro, embracing whole clumps of figures, shouting out hellos at the top of his lungs. Clearly, these were people he knew and liked, whom he hadn't seen for a great many years.

"Saved my life, they did," he explained to Eric, in between greetings. "I was pretty well broke up after coming down the spout that first time. By sheer good luck, I stumbled into this grove, thinking, I suppose, to curl up and die in peace. But these dear old sticks took pity on me. They nursed and sheltered and generally rustled me back to life."

A long applauselike rustle followed this speech. The tree-figures were tremendously pleased to see the old man, though rather hampered, Eric observed, by their stiff postures. They moved ever so slowly, reaching out to greet their friend. They nodded their heads and swiveled their bodies inch by arduous inch, then toiled valiantly to recover their positions.

The fishcatcher was respectful throughout these rather ridiculous gymnastics and did not mind at all the long waits and awkward pauses in-between. When the first round of hellos was completed, he cried out eagerly to the grove, "And now! Let me introduce you to my traveling companion." So Eric was taken between and around large numbers of twiggish arms, and he shook hands when they were laboriously offered, and tried to understand what was being said to him. And after a while, he did understand. Within the drawn-out rustle were slow-spoken words, perfectly clear when you slowed your own ear to receive them.

"I . . . am . . . Wilmer . . . Diggs . . . sea . . . farer . . . swept . . . down . . . the . . . spout . . . in . . . a . . . hurr . . . i . . . cane . . . in . . . nine . . . teen . . . thir . . . ty . . . six. . . ."

"I . . . . . am . . . . . Su . . . . . san . . . . . Ratch . . . . . fish . . . . . catch . . . . . er . . . . . caught . . . . . in . . . . . the . . . . . whirl . . . . . pool . . . . . chas . . . . . ing . . . . . blue . . . . fish . . . . . eight . . . . . een . . . . . twen . . . . . ty . . . . . one. . . ."

"Here . . . . be . . . . Cap . . . . tain . . . . Dav . . . . id . . . . Jones . . . . trad . . . . er . . . . blown . . . . off . . . . course . . . . by . . . . a . . . . blast . . . . ed . . . . ty . . . . phoon . . . . and . . . . swal . . . . lowed . . . . up . . . . ship . . . . and . . . . all. . . ."

"Tell him what year, Davy," said the fishcatcher, who was listening with interest to these recitations.

"Six . . . . teen . . . . sev . . . . en . . . . ty . . . . two," came the slowest of all the slow-rustling voices, and Zeke Cantrip turned to Eric with a triumphant grin.

"That's more than three hundred years ago. There are others here older, but none whom we can any longer understand. The distance between their words has become so great that whole days may pass (by our Twillian measure) before a single sentence is uttered. Among those here in the settlement, it makes no difference, of course. Slow or fast, it's all the same. You can be sure that conversations are under way even now that we cannot detect, conversations that may require hundreds or thousands of years to complete. Our ears hear only the youngest, quickest voices, those still in the range of our time-tempered senses."

"Do you mean that the longer they're here, the slower they go?" Eric whispered. He didn't want to embarrass the members of the settlement.

"Yes, it's true! And nothing to be ashamed of!" the fishcatcher answered. "People here are proud of their age. The long-range view is much prized in the settlement, and difficult to achieve, especially coming from a background of short-term struggle and risk. It takes hundreds of timeless years before the slowdown is complete. By that time, of course, the short-range view has paid the price. I'm told by my friends here that the present becomes so small and insignificant, so uninteresting in the general scheme of things, that it tends to become completely ignored. Ahem!"

Here the fishcatcher suddenly did see fit to lower his voice, and to draw Eric closer to him. "There are some particularly ancient members of this settlement," he whispered, "who do not even see us because of the unimaginably long and timeless range of their view. To them, you and I simply do not exist!"

Eric looked around skeptically. But catching sight of a hulking tree whose primeval limbs snarled and bristled in a rather threatening way, he stepped closer to Mr. Cantrip.

"The same force is at work on us even as we speak," the fishcatcher went on cheerfully. "You may have noticed the difficulty we had hiking cross-country, and your sea gull's courageous attempts to fly. We are all suffering the effects of timelessness. Our words are slowing, our motions are becoming fewer, our feet are beginning to take root in the ground, just as the inhabitants here have rooted and stiffened and disappeared altogether in some cases under layers of tree bark. It's Underwhirl's changeless core working to hold us still, to lengthen our view."

Eric had been glancing about during the last part of this explanation. Now he interrupted in excitement. "Do you suppose my parents could be here somewhere? They were swept away in a storm like many of these others. And were never seen again!"

"You can go around and look if you wish," the fishcatcher replied, "but it's not very likely, I'm afraid. The folks you see here are the lucky few who survived the drop. For every one of them, hundreds of others perished on the trip down. Or, what's more probable, they perished in the sea and never made it into the whirlpool at all."

Despite these discouraging words, Eric insisted on

examining each and every one of the grove's inhabitants, unless they had entirely vanished behind bark.
He questioned those who could be questioned and
checked the fringes of the settlement for recent arrivals.
(His parents would have looked like spring chickens
in this venerable crowd.) But in the end, he came
away with nothing and sank down on the ground so
sadly and limply that the fishcatcher was alarmed and
spoke up.

"Listen here, young fellow. It takes a rare caliber of
traveler to navigate the spouts to Underwhirl. You
should be proud that you yourself have managed,
though it was with the help of an old hand like me."
The fishcatcher's eyes glittered.

"What's more, I have a return journey to think about
and can't take the chance of being weighted down by
a moper. It's a dangerous business, the return. Not
something any of these folks ever dreamed of trying."
He motioned at the firmly rooted settlement.

"And that's why I'd advise you to shake a leg, and
keep your eyes bright, and walk about whenever
possible," Mr. Cantrip went on in a louder voice. He
peered at Eric with more concern. "And don't be caught
napping if you want to get back to Twill!" he shouted.

Unaccountably, Eric was nodding off. A blissful
tiredness was invading his bones. The old man's voice
became a buzz in his ear. He lay back in the grass
between tree roots and gazed through the boughs at
the sky. The lampfish were there, drifting about. Once
again Eric was soothed by their peacefulness and envied

them the safety of this extraordinary world so far from Twill. He was about to close his eyes and dive head first into a long and delicious sleep when—

"The gull! The gull! Something's wrong with the gull!" Mr. Cantrip's voice rang out like a bell.

Good grief, what a jolt! Eric had completely forgotten Sir Gullstone since their arrival at the settlement. Now his eyes alighted upon a heap of feathers fallen in the midst of the grove. It was a heap that, even as Eric watched, made a painful leap into the air and crashed to the ground like a broken kite.

"Oh, no! Gully!"

"That's the trouble with birds. They never give up," Zeke remarked, as Eric rushed wildly to the sea gull's side. "The poor thing's been slamming himself around ever since we got here. He's not going to last very long at this rate. We may have to cast off sooner than I'd planned."

"He's not a poor thing and he is going to last!" Eric practically screamed as he knelt on the ground. He picked up Gullstone and set him on his feet, but the big bird winced and cried out and jumped away. Then he crouched down and gave Eric a hard look.

"He's hurt somewhere! That's what he does when he's hurt."

"It's his wing, most likely," the fishcatcher said, "from trying so hard to fly. If you can get your hands around him, I'll take a closer look. There's a way to make a splint that might do him some good."

So Eric approached Gullstone and tried to take him

in his arms, but the bird got away and hid in a bush.
From the bush he fled behind Captain David Jones and
nestled in his roots. And from there he ran squawking
out of the grove, and though he did not move very
fast, Eric moved slower; it was apparent that Underwhirl's insidious slowing process was very much at work
on them both.

Gullstone had panicked by now. He could not stop
hurling himself forward even after Eric had dropped
behind and halted. On and on he ran, appearing briefly
on rises, then vanishing into dips in the land and reap-
pearing further off. His anguished cries traveled back
to Eric. The bird was trying to launch himself again,
despite the wound in his wing.

"No, Gully. Stop that! Come back here. We'll fix it."

He would not come. When Eric looked around for
the fishcatcher, he saw that the old man had abandoned
the chase. He was crouched on the ground just outside
the settlement, and with his head thrown back, he was
shouting at the sky. What he shouted Eric could not
hear, because his voice was erased by the weighty distance between them. In the other direction, Gully's cries
were being muffled, too. They grew fainter as the bird
moved further away.

"Help!" Eric shrieked. "Gullstone's going off!" The
fishcatcher could not hear him and paid no attention.
As Eric watched, he stood up and raised his arms slowly
into the air, assuming the same powerful stance as he
had on the high rock that morning when the lampfish
at Dead Man's Point was killed. He appeared to be
conjuring or calling for something.

And then Eric saw that he was being answered. One of the lampfish was dropping toward the ground. It moved in Mr. Cantrip's direction and hovered for a moment, blimplike, over his head. Then the fish dropped the remaining feet to the ground and cut off Eric's view of the old man. A moment later, it rose. But when its body cleared the ground—Eric stared in horror—Mr. Cantrip had disappeared. He no longer stood where he had been, nor was he anywhere around the settlement.

The lampfish went up lightly into the air. It drifted away, becoming lost in a rosy flotilla of other fish. A long and dreadful silence followed. Looking down, Eric found himself alone upon the vast sweep of Underwhirl's landscape. He turned toward the rise where the gull had last appeared.

"Gully! Please come back!"

There was no movement there, or anywhere in the whole unchanging land. And though he tried to go after the bird with brave bursts of running and walking, it wasn't long before Eric also became a stationary part of the view. The weight of the place overwhelmed him. He could not even retrace his steps to the settlement, for what little use that might have been. Without Gullstone, it no longer mattered where or when or how he was. He dropped down to rest for the third or thirteenth or thirtieth time (it was impossible to keep track) and in the end he simply could not get up.

15

EVERY once in a while, Eric yelled, "Gully!" Or, "Zeke, you rat! Come back this minute!" Or, despairingly as time passed, "I'm here. Here!"

Time was not really passing, he reminded himself, because nothing passed in Underwhirl. It was his own mind that made time seem to pass, that had learned time so well, it could not stop dividing before from after, now from then—even when there was nothing left to divide.

He yelled to let off steam.

"Aunt Opal! Mrs. Holly! Here I am!" Up in Twill, his voice would have made some mark, even if his aunt hadn't heard. A gull flapping by might have looked at him warily. An echo might have started up. The air might have vibrated a little. An ant might have scuttled away. Here in this unmoving countryside, his yells left no trace of having been. Nothing received the noise and nothing reacted. Or if, somewhere, something heard, it paid no attention. It ignored him in the same way the ancient trees in the settlement had ignored him, because he was small and short-lived and their attention was fixed on the long-range view.

Eric turned his face to the sky. Overhead, schools of lampfish streamed and floated. Sometimes they came together in clumps; sometimes they drifted apart. Sometimes they were high up and small to the eye; sometimes they dropped low, eclipsing half the sky. Aimless they looked, mindless and meaningless, and yet Eric wondered if there wasn't some pattern at work up there, some rhythm or order that might help him if he could only see it. It was the way of things in Underwhirl, he was beginning to understand. The pattern might not be easy to detect. In some cases, like the long-range tree conversations, it might be beyond the reach of ordinary, time-ridden senses. But, maybe, if he looked long enough, a key would emerge. Even now, sharpening his eyes, he noticed something interesting. Scattered as the lampfish appeared, they were all moving in a similar direction.

Eric sat up. As he watched, a haphazard mass made up of hundreds of fish began to assume peculiar forms in the sky. The sprawl gathered into a luscious-looking cream puff shape, then became a potbellied stove, then rounded again into a flushed moon that gradually began to flatten. Meanwhile, through all these transformations, the fish continued to drift in a counterclockwise direction. Their rotation was picking up speed.

Eric got to his feet. Now the rosy bodies were overlapped and beginning to blend together. Round and round the lampfish flew, their great mustaches rippling and entangling, whipping up the air. A light breeze blew down and crossed Eric's cheek.

"Wind!" he cried, and reached his hand up for more.

There was more. In no time, a small gale was blowing across Underwhirl's lands, and the lampfish had become a glowing wheel of current in the sky. Eric's hair whirled around his head. He swept it back from his eyes and shouted with excitement. After the weight, the terrible stillness of Underwhirl, these old feelings of sweep and swirl, of drag and pull, seemed almost unbearably thrilling.

But something else was beginning to happen. The revolving wheel was changing. Its center was falling in, dropping with a funnel-like shape toward the ground while the rim went on spinning high above. Down and down came the whirling form, nosing here and there in a shortsighted way, as if it were searching for something. Eric knew what it was by now. He cried out for Gully one last time and, though the wind was strong, raised his arms in the air.

In a moment, quite gently considering the turbulence, he felt himself lifted. He rose off the ground and was held briefly at some calm center, as if his weight were being assessed and a certain balance sought. Then—*whoosh*—he was drawn upward, and though he knew that many lampfish surrounded him, they seemed to meld before his eyes into one great body that spun and spun him rosily up the spout.

For that was what it was, of course. The spout. The

whirlpool. Even as Eric watched, it began to take more recognizable shape around him. He saw how its energy came from the lampfish alone, how their powerful swirl set a current in motion that drove up toward Twill like a furious drill. So, it was the lampfish who'd kept the channel open all these years, playing against the moon and the upper world's rule of change. Lights the fish were, yes. And guides when need be. But before all else, they'd made the spouts for themselves. To escape from Underwhirl, Eric guessed, just as he was doing now. To break the iron grip of their world and rise up to the wild, free currents above. But, what was that?

"Gully?"

A vague outline of something was paddling toward him. He saw the glimmer of a feather, the golden flash of an eye. A rubbery *thunk, thunk* reached his ears, as of tarpaulin moving through water.

"Mr. Cantrip! Is that you?"

"Ahoy! Ahoy!" came the answer, and Eric's heart leaped. It was both, man and bird! They were approaching side by side along the spout's slow-turning wall. Since this was now composed almost entirely of seawater, there was much floundering and not a little coughing and sputtering as the three came joyfully together.

"Watch the gull!" Zeke warned. "He's torn his wing. I had the devil of a time trying to find him down there. He'd crept into a hole and couldn't be spied from the air."

"But where were you!" Eric demanded, angrily. "You left me all alone."

The old man shook his head and addressed himself to Gullstone, who had rushed headlong for Eric at the first sight of him and now crouched snugly inside his arm.

"How do you like that for a show of thanks? Here I perform miracles of search, find, and escape, and the boy complains about a few minutes left alone."

"A few minutes! It was hours," Eric said. "Or maybe even days. What were you doing going up in that fish? You made a spell, didn't you. I saw it happen."

"Up? Spell? What do you mean? You're making me sound like some small-time wizard." The fishcatcher winked at Gully, who gave Eric the sort of unreadable yellow stare that sea gulls are famous for.

"Gully! You're no help at all! Whose side are you on anyway?"

Next, Zeke Cantrip was struck by another infuriating case of deafness. He would not hear a single word put to him, though Eric was dying to report his discovery about the lampfish and the spout, and to press the old man for more systems and schemes. Flocks of new ideas were rising in his mind, and new explanations for things he had seen in Underwhirl. But suddenly, there was no time to interrogate Zeke anyway, or even to feel relief at having escaped that leaden land. The spout had begun to spin faster.

All the while, the group had been slowly ascending with the current, moving around and up the bowl-shaped wall of the whirlpool. When Eric looked down, he saw the rosy glow of the Underwhirl lampfish shining up toward them. The fish had stopped rising and were now being left behind. As their warm light receded, the water itself cooled and then turned cold.

Looking ahead, Eric saw the watery walls over his head begin to churn and race, to bulge and tear loose from the confinement of their sides. These renegade surges crashed together, producing clouds of spray. Higher up, when the spray cleared, Eric could see mountainous swells and waves flying toward one another. They smashed together with such terrific force that the vibrations shivered the whole of the spout's tremendous bowl.

Beside him, the fishcatcher clutched his arm. "Now, Eric," he said, "final instructions before the fray. And listen carefully, for we've arrived amidst a storm."

The old man's face had turned as gray as the water around them, Eric saw. There was no sign of his usual teasing and good humor.

"It's Twill, isn't it? We're coming home."

"Aye, Twill. What else? Our marvelous coast." The trace of a giggle flicked through his voice. Eric grabbed his shoulder.

"Tell me quickly," he said. "Say what we need to do."

Zeke Cantrip wet his lips and gazed for a moment at Gullstone. Then he spoke, low and fast.

"First, expect no help from the big fish above. They are as much at the mercy of Twill's storms as you, and must guard themselves. A dwindling species they are, and know it all too well. Those who die above are replaced by those below, but in Underwhirl, as you have seen, nothing new is ever made. The cloudfish there are the last of the lot. Where they once rose in droves to our restless upper world, now they replace themselves frugally, one by one. So many in these later years have been killed."

Over their heads, two giant waves collided and broke, sending strong ripples down the walls of the whirlpool.

"What else," cried Eric. "Quick. Hurry!"

"Don't try to hold the bird," the fishcatcher went on. "He's hurt already and would certainly be crushed by your arms when the big waves start. Let him go as he will, this time above all others. As for you, move with the swirl—don't pit yourself against it. And if you make the ocean's surface, howl and rage toward the sky."

"Howl and rage!" said Eric. "But why? What shall I howl?"

"Anything!" shouted the fishcatcher. The current was beginning to carry them upward faster, and to drown out his voice. "Yell, scream, and shriek! The trick is to be heard, to show them where you are."

"Who?" shouted Eric. "There'll be no one out in this!" Despite the old man's warning, he drew Gullstone against his chest.

The waves were turning fierce. Mr. Cantrip was rolled away from them. He was tossed and turned around like a twig in a gale, and sucked out of sight and thrown near them again. Gullstone screeched when he saw this, and beat his wings, breaking Eric's grasp.

Then, finding himself suddenly airborne, he veered toward the fishcatcher. He landed with a squawk on his shoulder and clung with all his strength.

"Away, you crazy bird. There's no use staying with me!" the old man roared, trying to knock him off. "Save the boy, do you hear? Go and gather the crew. Fly off and bring them here. Fly, I say! Fly!"

"No, Gully! Come!" Eric cried in a panic. Even as he did, a wave bore down on them from above. Gullstone flapped weakly into the air as it broke over their heads. Eric was blinded by a tremendous gush of surf and felt himself thrown and twisted and dragged through the water. When he got his eyes open again, the bird was nowhere in sight and the fishcatcher had been cast a great distance away.

"Mr. Cantrip!" he choked out. The waves were driving them apart. "Zeke! Where's Gully?"

In answer, over the crashing water, Eric heard a sound more terrifying than the roar of any storm. Faint it was at first, just an intermittent chuckle and hoot. But gradually the laughter broadened and grew continuous, and as the fit came full force upon the old man, he twisted and shrieked in the waves and seemed barely able to keep himself afloat. Finally, from far across the water, a voice rang out powerfully above the water and wind.

"Farewell!" it cried. "Till we meet again!" And then, from further away, "Keep your eye on the sky!"

After this, there were no more sounds, though Eric yelled repeatedly and begged for an answer. He was in grave danger, often so buried in the troughs of waves that he could not tell up from down. Whenever he could, he gave a shout in what he thought to be the skyward direction. But he was out of breath most of the time, always gasping for air before the next terrible wave.

"Rage!" the fishcatcher had said. "Howl! Show them where you are!" But how can you rage when a sea rises against you? At such times, it is hard enough simply to stay afloat.

By now, Eric had come out on what he supposed must be the ocean's surface. The air was so full of salt spray and the swells were so mountainous that at first he did not see how wide the sky had spread overhead. He was being pushed away from the whirlpool's center, however, and the fury of the water was beginning to die down. Not that he was out of danger. His strength was failing, and his arms and legs had turned numb from the frigid water. He was more at risk than ever of sinking under the waves, and in another few minutes might well have given up and let himself go. But his blurry eyes spied something in the sky. It came through the gray storm clouds and raced toward him. A huge flapping bird it appeared to be at first. But as the creature approached, Eric saw that it was composed more of belly than wing and was accompanied by numbers of small winged figures that flew at its head and along its flanks.

Winged figures! Eric closed his eyes and looked again. Underwhirl's weird sights had certainly rearranged his mind. They were plain and ordinary sea gulls, of course!

"Here! I'm here!" he tried to yell.

The formation passed over him and went on to circle the whirlpool's center. Now Eric saw that the strange bellied creature was none other than a big net held aloft in the bills of at least a hundred gulls. It slapped and blew in the storm winds as it went over the spout.

"Help!" Eric cried, waving feebly. He felt comforted to know that Gullstone had fought through to Mr. Cantrip's crew. The bird, at least, was safe on dry land. As for Eric, he was beginning to sink. His arms and legs were rebelling. They refused to move when he issued an order.

"Swim!" he commanded. They lay like logs in the water. "Thrash!" he cried. They settled lower and limper. It was as if he no longer had charge of his body, as if he were a captain doomed to go down with the ship. And he did go down! He had just slipped under the water when three scout gulls caught sight of him and alerted the net carriers with squawks.

In seconds, they were above him, dropping the net, scooping him up. Compared to a lampfish, he must have seemed featherlight. He came out of the water with a zip and a flash. And though, afterward, Eric tried to remember his remarkable trip to shore, and even imagined looking down gratefully at Twill's foaming coast, in fact he saw nothing more that day than the inside of his own eyelids. He did not get six feet into the air before he passed dead out from exhaustion and fright.

16

"**E**RIC?" The voice blew toward him across a dark plain. There was something familiar about it.

"Eric!" For one heart-stopping moment, he thought it was his mother come to fetch him at last in the cabin by the sea. Then he remembered that she was dead, and with a sad sigh he allowed himself to drift away out of hearing again.

"Eric!"

The voice would not let him go. It sounded rather irritable, as if it was his turn to cook supper and he'd come home late again.

"Hello, Aunt Opal. Here I am at last."

"Well, I should say you are! And not in the best condition either." This remark came from a second voice sounding twice as irritable as the first.

"The Blaster had his hands on you, there's no doubt he did," this voice continued. "Took your boots, tore your shirt. And what are these nasty old socks he's stuck onto your feet? I guess you'll be careful after this what you say about him. It's a warning, no less."

"Hello, Mrs. Holly," said Eric, opening his eyes. He tried to smile at her, and at his aunt. Never had he seen two whiter faces staring into his.

"Well! Harrumph!" They could not bring themselves to hug him yet. They had been so frightened. Now they were in a rage.

"It's a good thing you washed up when you did, or we, personally, would've come out and drowned you!" Mrs. Holly announced. Eric really did smile at this. It was how he always felt after Gullstone came through danger. He glanced around the room. He was lying on his own bed.

"Where's Gully?" he asked. "Asleep near the fire, I bet. He's the one who almost drowned. We went down Cantrip's Spout."

An odd bubble came up his throat as he said this, and he thought for a minute that he was going to start laughing.

"We had given you up for lost," Aunt Opal said. "Some fishcatchers found you this morning cast up on Strangle Beach after the storm. It's been three days, Eric, since you disappeared at sea. You were sighted, you know, out alone rowing after dark, heading toward the whirlpool with a flock of gulls." She looked at him doubtfully. "It didn't sound like you."

"It was," Eric assured her. "But I wasn't alone. Zeke Cantrip was with me, and you won't believe what we saw out there. Lampfish! Coming up the spout! And that was just the beginning. Wait until you hear about our trip to Underwhirl. And the tree settlement, and the clouds that turned out to be lamps. What about Mr. Cantrip, by the way?" He raised himself on one elbow. "Has he turned up onshore yet?"

Mrs. Holly's mouth fell open at this, for old Cantrip was years dead, as anyone in his right mind knew.

"Stop garbling your words," she snapped. "I can hardly understand what you say."

Aunt Opal bent forward and put her hand on his forehead. "Don't push yourself," she murmured. "You've had a terrible ordeal. Just lie back and sleep. You'll be better soon."

"But I am better," Eric insisted. "There's nothing wrong with me at all. I only wanted to know if Zeke Cantrip was rescued. By his gull crew. They were the ones who rescued me, in Zeke's big net when I came up the spout. Do you know that it's the lampfish that have caused our whirlpools? They spin themselves up here to escape from Underwhirl, though every one knows what the end must be."

This simple speech produced such dismayed expressions on the faces in front of him that Eric couldn't help laughing.

Mrs. Holly turned pale and backed away several steps.

"He's been touched!" she shrieked. "It's the whirlpool, all right. I've never heard such a twisting of words in my life. Or such cackling. Except once before," she added, in an ominous lower tone.

"Eric!" cried his aunt. "Take hold of yourself. There is nothing funny about Cantrip's Spout."

"It's not the spout," Eric cried, "but coming home! It's seeing both how alive and how deadly Twill is, and feeling the back and forth pull of its tides. And the swirl!"

With this, he jumped off his bed and began a strange circling walk. Round and round he went, moving clockwise, dodging the furniture in the room at first, then tramping straight through it as the pace of his rounds increased. Mrs. Holly fled to the kitchen when she saw how it was.

"Opal! Come away. He's as mad as old Zeke. It's The Blaster's handiwork. Come! Come away!" With a final shriek, the front door was thrown open, and there was a clatter of rapidly departing feet.

But Aunt Opal stood her ground, bristly pine tree that she was, and sat on the end of Eric's bed to wait for the walking fit to pass. When it did, she drew him back to bed, and tucked him in. She told him not to mind Mrs. Holly, the silly old goose. Whatever was wrong with him, it was sure to come right soon. She was only glad to have him back safe, and besides she didn't put much stock in other people's opinions, as he knew quite well. This was his home, wasn't it? He must stay and be cared for, Old Blaster or not. She wanted him to know that he'd always be welcome no matter where he'd been or what had happened or how he talked. (She paused for breath and looked at him with great fondness, but also a bit of uneasiness.) No matter what terrible thing happened next.

"What do you mean, 'terrible thing'?" Eric demanded, sitting up in alarm. There was something odd about her tone. "What terrible thing? I want to know!"

"Eric," she said, in the softest of voices, "Gullstone's still out. He never came home."

THERE WAS no doubt where the big bird would be. Strangle Beach was the place broken things washed ashore. Its shape caught them up, as the fish-catcher had said.

"The crazy gull must have tried to fly back with the crew," Eric exclaimed, reaching for his clothes. "He never knows when to stop. He tore his wing in Underwhirl by always trying to fly."

For all her sympathy, Aunt Opal could not see what he meant.

"Crew?" she repeated, as if his mind was confused. "Under-what, did you say? Why shouldn't a bird fly, I'd like to know? Look here, I strongly recommend clam broth and bed rest!"

Despite her protests, Eric was out the door two minutes later. He might have gotten to Strangle Point even faster except for his boots. They were an outgrown pair dragged from the back of his trunk, and they pinched his feet fiercely on the run across the fields.

"Gullstone. Wait!"

Why he yelled that, he didn't know. He came to the edge of the rise and looked down. His eyes were as sharp as a hunting hawk's. The small, drab mound on the beach below would have been invisible to anyone else.

"Wait for me, Gully. I'm coming!" he screamed.

The amazing thing was, the gull did wait. How he managed to hang on, torn apart that way, smashed and rolled across the sand, Eric never knew. He'd always had unusual strength. He'd come through so many storms before.

"All right, Gully. It's me. I'm here."

The beach was still windy, the surf high. Sand blew through the air. Clumps of dirty foam quivered like jelly in wet hollows. Gullstone had been thrown in a hollow of his own. Luckily the tide was falling. The waves left them alone.

"Don't move until I see what to do," Eric said, then bit his lip when he saw the mangled wing. The dark stains in the sand underneath weren't from salt water or rain. "There is something twisted in your back, I think. There's a rather deep gash on the side of your neck." His voice seemed, suddenly, not to belong to him. It kept reporting things he didn't want to see. "And your leg is broken, and your stomach is scratched. Well, not scratched exactly, more . . ."

When he saw what more, he drew the gull all together in the middle of his arms and sealed his lips against the voice. He held Gully gently, so he'd know he didn't have to wait anymore. He could go when he wanted. He, Eric, would let him go, because you can't hold back what has to go on. The fishcatcher had said that, and he was right. There was no one who wanted to go on more than Gullstone at that moment. Even so, the faithful bird did not like to disappoint. When,

at last, his powerful lungs began to falter, he gazed at
his friend with such shame and distress in his lemon-
colored eyes, that Eric's heart nearly broke.

"It's all right, Gully," he told him, tears slipping
down from his eyes. He touched his cheek to the great
feathered head. "I'm letting you go, anytime you want.
Anytime," Eric wept. "Go ahead. Go."

THEY BURIED Sir Gullstone in a high field just
back of the Strangle Point ledges. In the rain. Without
the fishcatcher. He didn't turn up. Eric looked and
looked.

"He said we'd meet again, and I hope it's soon," he
told the gull crew in a trembling voice between shovel
loads of dirt. "There are quite a few things that need
to be explained."

Eric hadn't expected to have help from the birds.
But there was the crew, every last one of them, sitting
on the roof of the fishcatcher's shack as he came, stag-
gering under Gully's weight, up the rocky path from
Strangle Point beach. They knew what had happened.
Every sea gull knows when another has fallen. And
when Eric laid Gully's body down on the shack's front
stoop, every gull on the roof came forward to look.
Some flew down and walked distractedly about.

They had been waiting for the fishcatcher, too, Eric
saw. The yard was littered with droppings and jimmied
mussel shells. The shack had the smell of a closed-up
place. While every gull watched, Eric marched in the
door, lit a kerosene lamp, and held it over his head.

"I need a box," he announced to those milling near the door. More birds fluttered to the ground. They gathered around the stoop and looked up at the sky. It was beginning to rain again.

"A tight, covered box," Eric said, hearing the drops on the roof. His own eyes were in a state of constant overflow.

Outside, the gulls strutted and stretched their wings, and with odd clucks and whoops seemed to conference among themselves. Then, as if some decision had been reached, the flock moved over to surround an ancient tackle shed in the yard. In moments, they had set up such a rasping chorus of bleats and caws that Eric came to investigate the trouble. And there, in the shed, he found a fine wood box of the sort that long ago might have held exotic tea.

Gullstone's body was arranged inside with such attention to detail (every feather was made clean and straight) that it also gathered strangeness and a foreign air. When, before shutting the lid, Eric paused to look one final time, he saw that Gullstone really had gone off somewhere. The bird was no more in that box than any one of them. After this, he was able to take steadier breaths. He nailed the lid down with solid strokes and didn't worry that there was anything left trapped inside.

The rain was falling continuously now, and when the place for the grave had been chosen, and the hole had been dug, and the fine box put into it and covered with earth, all hands returned in silence to the shack. Eric fired up the creaky wood stove and made a kettle hot for tea. He placed candles in the one window, as many as he could find, and lit them all at once as tradition required. Anyone who wanted to laugh at him for making a weep for a bird, could laugh. Fortunately, there was no one of that sort about.

The gull crew did not hesitate to accept his invitation to come indoors. They perched in orderly groups on various antique prods and barrels and nets around the room, and respectfully eyed some bins of dried fish that the old man had put aside for the Season of Storms.

In fact, everything necessary for a long, comfortable evening, and for many evenings, was there somewhere in that jumbly place. So much so, that Eric decided to stay on for a while. He dispensed with the time-consuming business of feeding the Old Blaster, and they all, despite their gloom, munched on biscuits and left-over fish stew, along with a well-cured salami found hanging beneath the eaves.

"I don't think Zeke would mind putting us up for a few days, under the circumstances, do you?" Eric asked the gulls. They glanced about, as if they thought the fellow might appear at any time. Surrounded on all sides by the old man's weird collection, Eric also felt his nearness, but with such a mixture of emotions that he hardly knew what his true feelings were. For sometimes, thinking of their adventure, it seemed that he'd been in the hands of a wily trickster who was out for a bit of sport. And other times, his companion had seemed a wise traveler and friend. And then again he remembered the man's horrible giggling and periods of madness, and at the same time his plain fishcatcher's humor and humble ways.

He recalled his shaky legs and his treacherous cape, his honest advice and his deceptive ears. Above all, the picture that haunted Eric was of Zeke Cantrip standing tall with his powerful arms lifted toward the sky. But this was such an unsettling memory, and raised such disturbing questions about the fishcatcher's real identity, that he pushed it aside. There was only one way to find out what everything meant, how the confusing pieces of their journey added up, and that was to speak to the fishcatcher again.

"I suppose he must have known where he was taking us all along," Eric said to the crew. "And yet . . ." He paused and, thinking of Gully, he shook his head in disbelief, and his eyes filled with bitter tears.

The fishcatcher did not come to Gullstone's weep that night, nor did he appear the day after, or the next day, or the next. While they waited, Eric and the crew did odd jobs around the shack or went fishing for Aunt Opal if the weather permitted. The season had now officially changed. Rough seas were the rule off Twill's rocky coast. The sky was often dark and foreboding, and The Blaster was much on people's minds. When would he strike? Whom would he snatch?

The muttering on street corners began in town again. Eric saw small groups of townsfolk gathered when he came in to buy supplies. He noticed heads turn as he passed by, and saw suspicious, half-frightened glances sent his way. Since his return up the spout, there'd been no friendly words or congratulations.

"They haven't started calling their dogs home yet, but I think it's only a matter of time," he told Aunt Opal one evening during a visit to her cabin. "For some reason, they've linked me up with The Blaster in their minds. It's superstition of the silliest kind."

"Mrs. Holly, I'm afraid, has spread a bit of gossip," she replied. "We're not speaking, at the moment, on that account. But Eric, if you'd only consider coming back here to live, we might fix things up. It's staying out there by yourself with those birds that has folks comparing you to one who went before."

"To Zeke Cantrip, you mean."

"Well . . ." Aunt Opal dropped an uncomfortable glance toward his feet. There were many resemblances; she could not say there weren't. "Those very boots you're wearing have a strange look to them. Where'd you come across a peculiar pair like that?"

"They're old ones of Zeke's," he said, while she turned a paler shade. "To tide me over, that's all. He'll want them again if he ever comes home."

He could not go back to live with Aunt Opal. He was different now. Everything was changed. He missed Gullstone badly and often walked the slippery ledges, glaring at the sea. The spout spun there, reminding him of Underwhirl. On moonless evenings, the lampfish rose and glowed, or swam in their marvelous caldrons of light. Then Eric felt a strong wish to go out among them again, and to look back at Twill from their alien sea. Perhaps, after all, he was a traveler at heart. Like the rosy-hued fish, he'd acquired a taste for risk.

He liked to listen to the surf crash on the beach at night. The wind in his face, the spray from a wave, the roar of water over rock—after Underwhirl he liked to hear and see and feel all these, all the time. In blacker moods, he wished The Blaster would get on with his game of slowly blowing Twill apart. Eric longed for a storm, a great violent swirl. But the old tyrant was playing particularly sly and cruel that year, holding off on his attack for weeks beyond the usual time. Everyone in Twill was on tenterhooks. Every loose object had been hammered or cinched or cleated to the ground. The sheds had been reinforced. The boats were triple moored. Twickham's weather windows were boarded up and nailed tight.

By day, fishcatching families kept their dories close to shore and appointed the younger children to stand watch on the cliffs. At night, every sleeper slept with half an open ear. Nerves grew taut. Patience ran out. And still The Blaster held back and away.

And then one morning, there he was, just creeping with his capes into the eastern sky. ("Help!" screeched Mrs. Holly, flying into her house.) He turned the clouds in his path the lurid purples of a bruise. He lurched out over the ocean with arrogant tread and fired a lightning bolt and unleashed gale winds.

The people of Twill were in such a state of nerves by this time that they screamed and trampled one another trying to get inside. Some even went so far as to alert their neighbors by ringing the lampfish bells, which thereafter became a common practice along the coast and led directly to the construction of the many odd-shaped but enormous bell towers for which Twill's coast, in later years, was known in the world.

Out on Strangle Point, Eric called Zeke's gulls together and ordered a general battening down of shack and yard. The birds were devoted to him now and did everything he said. Then he directed the crew indoors and issued generous rations of dried fish from the bins. He asked for cooperation and consideration for others in close quarters, and when order seemed at least on the verge of prevailing (everyone was quite jumpy), he slipped out the cabin door and made for the ledges.

The storm had struck full force by now, and the sea had been whipped to a fury known only on the coast of Twill. The air was filled with the thunder of surf and the whine of wind. Eric was knocked down twice, making his way across the field. So vicious was the gale that his coat was peeled off his back and up his arms and flew high into the branches of a nearby plane tree, where it thrashed and flapped like a mad bird.

Anyone watching him might now have decided that some madness had descended on Eric as well. Without his coat, he fought on across the field. He paused by Sir Gullstone's grave, then moved across to a rocky cliff. Here he stood and scowled down at the beach, leaning at such a reckless angle that he seemed to be taunting The Blaster himself to blow him over. And perhaps, in another minute, a giant windy hand would have come along and done the job, but at that moment, the waves cast two black, soggy items up on the sand below. Eric straightened up and sharpened his gaze. Shoes, they appeared to be. No. A pair of boots!

He was off the ledge in a flash, dropping down a steep place between the rocks to the beach or, rather, to such beach as was left. The tide was rising, and foaming breakers careened wildly up the shore. But there, yes, at the high-water mark lay two abandoned boots.

"My boots!" screamed Eric. With an ecstatic leap he snagged them, and drew them safely from the waves' reach. Then he raised them up in the air to thank the fishcatcher—for certainly the old rascal was at the bottom of this! It only went to prove that he was still out there somewhere.

"Ahoy!" shouted Eric into the teeth of the gale. "Come back, Mr. Cantrip! Please come back soon!"

At this, the wind gave out an oddly familiar series of giggles, and a large and thoroughly terrifying wave roared forward and deposited another item at Eric's feet.

It was a small, wet sea gull, its feathers swirled and plastered with sand. Even as Eric knelt to look, a tiny head turned fiercely to meet him, and two arrogant legs poked testily at the ground, and a sharp beak zipped forward and pecked him hard on the hand. ("Ow!" cried Eric. "Why'd you do that?") Then the whole miniature contraption rose up and began to limp off with lordly strides. Eric leaned over and snatched it into his arms before the next mountainous wave could sweep it away.

ABOUT THE AUTHOR

Janet Taylor Lisle's *Afternoon of the Elves* is a 1990 Newbery Honor Book. Her other novels are *The Great Dimpole Oak, The Dancing Cats of Applesap,* and *Sirens and Spies.*

She lives with her family in Montclair, New Jersey, and spends summers on the seacoast of Rhode Island, the inspiration for the setting of *The Lampfish of Twill.*